Adam-Leap-The-Mountain . . .
. . . a Navajo half-breed Indian born of the wilderness in
the Western plains of America — a man capable of killing
ruthlessly to survive . . .

Deborah . . .
. . . an English girl who has ventured into a savage land
and been befriended by gentle Quakers in the Wild West.
Then, horror strikes out of the lonely wilderness when the
Quaker missionaries are massacred. Surviving the attack,
Deborah finds her future safety can be guaranteed only as
the woman of Adam-Leap-The-Mountain, who has already proclaimed his desire for her at their chance meeting beside a waterfall.

How can she reconcile her strict Victorian upbringing
with life as an obedient Navajo squaw? A man and a
woman divided by civilization but bound by passions
older than time itself . . .

Moon of
Laughing Flame
Belinda Grey

MILLS & BOON LIMITED
London · Sydney · Toronto

First published in Great Britain 1980
by Mills & Boon Limited, 17-19 Foley Street,
London W1A 1DR

ISBN 0 263 73211 8

Filmset in 10 on 11 pt Plantin

Made and printed in Great Britain by
C. Nicholls & Company Ltd.,
The Philips Park Press, Manchester

CHAPTER
ONE

AT night the stars seemed close enough to touch and the air had a fragrance it lacked in the heat of the day. Deborah was supposed to sleep in the wagon with Mrs. Laycock and Charity, but sometimes she would creep out when they were asleep, roll herself in a blanket, and fall asleep under the brilliant stars with the little, sighing noises of the night all around her. Mr. Laycock slept under the wagon, rifle close to his hand. The rifle, as he had explained carefully, was for the killing of game only. Intruders were to be scared away by firing a shot into the air.

"Thee must understand that all human life is sacred," he had told her. "We never kill or injure fellow beings but turn the other cheek as the Lord bids us. That is one of the most abiding tenets of our Faith."

His deep-set eyes glowed with the conviction of his belief. Deborah had listened respectfully and wondered what they would all do if a band of marauding Indians who hadn't read the Bible chanced upon the wagon with its little group of five people.

But when she had voiced her fears to Mrs. Laycock the older woman had given her a mildly reproachful look. "Thee must have a little courage, Debbie. Why should the Indians attack us when we go to spread the Word? We have a mission to fulfil and we must set out with hope in our hearts."

"And rocks in our heads!" Jed Williams muttered.

Jed was not a member of the Society of Friends, but he was privately devoted to the Laycocks, even if he did sometimes sneak a slug of whisky or a chew of tobacco when his employers weren't looking. And he had the inestimable advantage of having already been on the Santa Fe trail. It had been twenty years before when he had been a young man eager to go west and make his fortune. Jed, however, had never made any money at all, and eventually he had drifted back to Kansas City where the Laycocks had taken him on as a general handyman.

"They're all quite mad, you know," he had confided to Deborah when the plans for the journey had first been discussed. "Mad as hatters! Off to preach the Gospel to the Utes! The Utes aren't interested in any Gospel."

"All the more reason why we must go to them," Mr. Laycock had said when Jed voiced his doubts more tactfully. "Those poor savages have never heard the Word. They are ripe for salvation."

"At least we could travel with one of the regular trains," Jed had argued. "There's safety in numbers."

"The only true safety is in the Lord," Mrs. Laycock said smilingly. Her smile saved her from being a plain woman, lighting up her sallow features until she looked more like the eager bride of sixteen years before, and less like the careworn wife who had followed her husband meekly from town to town, preaching the Word.

"Wagon trains are often attacked," Mr. Laycock said, with the confidence of complete ignorance, "because the Indians fear so many whites on the move at once. Now we represent no threat to them, so they will not harm us."

Incredibly, after two months on the trail, they were still unscathed. Deborah couldn't help wondering if Mr. Laycock had been right after all and the Lord was looking after them. Certainly Jed had never expected to get so far without mishap. Even the summer had been kind to them, with more rain than usual so that the waterholes were brimming. Plenty of fresh drinking water compensated for occasional muddy patches along the trail, and when the sun shone the grasslands were emerald.

They had seen no sign of Indians beyond some diggers who had come around to beg for salt and coffee, and slunk away, giggling, when Mr. Laycock had tried to engage them in some kind of conversation. At Fort Dodge, where they had stopped to take on fresh supplies, there had been a few squaws hanging about the main gates.

"Soldiers' whores," Jed had said, jerking his thumb towards them.

"What's that?" fourteen-year-old Charity had demanded, pricking up her ears.

"Nothing to interest you," Jed said shortly, but Deborah had craned her neck to watch the shawled figures.

At eighteen she was old enough to feel an intense curiosity about matters that were spoken of only in whispers by the modest Laycocks. Sometimes she even tried to imagine what it would be like to have a lover. It was unlikely that she would ever catch a husband, for quite apart from a mop of bright red hair and a pair of greenish eyes, both of which put her low in the beauty stakes, she had no blood kin and no dowry. And since the war between the States had started three years before, there had been a definite scarcity of eligible men.

They had stayed overnight at the fort and enjoyed the luxury of a real bath. One or two of the officers had their wives with them and Mrs. Laycock had been able to spend a pleasant hour in female gossip with women of her own age, but the two girls had been packed off early to bed. Jed had sloped off to the barracks, "to discuss the way the war was going", but judging from his bleary eyes and slightly unsteady gait the next morning he had drunk several toasts to victory.

At Fort Dodge the trail forked to west and south, the western track reaching out towards Pueblo, the southern one towards Santa Fe itself.

"We follow the south for about a hundred miles and then swing west again on to the old pony trail," Mr. Laycock said. "For part of the way we will follow the San Juan river."

He sounded cheerful and confident as if he knew exactly where he was going. What he would find when he got there and where "there" actually was, seemed to be a matter between himself and the Lord. "I shall know when I have reached my journey's end," he said.

"There'll be Utes standing in line for salvation, I suppose," Jed muttered, and stumped off to water the oxen, who stood with heads drooping patiently in the heat.

Although they were into September there was no sign of an autumn snap in the air, though as they left the grasslands behind and began to climb towards the distant peaks the nights were getting colder.

"Beyond the peaks is the Painted Desert," Mr. Laycock explained to them as they sat around in the shade of the wagon eating the scones that Mrs. Laycock had just baked. "The Utes live there. We will find them, I've no doubt."

"They'll probably find us first," Jed said gloomily.

"Are we going to live in the middle of the desert?" Charity asked, looking slightly apprehensive.

"We will live where the Lord sets us," her mother told her placidly.

It sounded rather vague and disheartening, Deborah thought, wiping sweat from her forehead with the back of her hand. The bright sunshine had increased her already numerous freckles, and her grey gown with its wide, white collar was limp and spotted from the heat. It had been more than a month before, and the going was slower now as they made their way up from the plains into the high passes that cut deep swathes into the sun-baked mountains.

"Debbie, there is a stream beyond the rock," Mrs. Laycock said. "Will thee rinse the plates?"

"Yes, of course." The girl rose at once, collected the tin plates and mugs, and carried them across the grassy space where they were camped to the narrow path that twisted down between high boulders to the stream beyond. The stream bubbled down into a small, clear pool fed by a waterfall and the high rocks about it afforded concealment.

Dipping the utensils in the running water, she shook each one and put it on the bank to dry. From above she could hear the faint murmur of the others as they stretched out for a rest. Certainly she wouldn't be missed for an hour.

Yielding to temptation, she went down the path to the pool and began to unlace the bodice of her dress and free her mass of hair from the white sunbonnet that shaded her eyes and the back of her neck from the glare. A few minutes later she stepped down into the water, suppressing a cry as the cold stung her flesh. The pool reached only to the tips of her breasts, but she ducked down until only her head showed and then leaped up, shaking the drops of water from her slim frame.

The bed of the pool was of firm white sand that yielded slightly to the pressure of her bare toes. Somewhere behind the rocks a bird called mockingly and she threw back her head and called back, mimicking the harsh cry. From a large flat stone at the edge of the pool a tiny lizard blinked its jewelled eyes at her, and slid lazily away, flicking its tail. She watched it go, her mouth widening into a smile. There was always something interesting to be seen, even among these high peaks. Tiny, brilliant flowers clung to the crevices of the rocks and more than once they had spotted maize and corn growing wild in the narrow valleys.

Leaning back against the sloping bank, Deborah closed her eyes and wriggled her toes contentedly. A shadow fell across her closed eyelids and she opened her eyes, blinking up into a hawk-nosed, red-brown face, the eyes slanting darkly above high cheekbones.

Too terrified to scream or move she stared up at him as he straddled the rock; his long legs encased in buckskins, broad shoulders straining the seams of a fringed leather shirt. His hair, so black that it gleamed blue, was drawn up into a tail on the crown of his head and tied with a red band. A bow was slung across his back and in one hand he carried a rifle. She had never seen anyone so magnificent or so frightening.

"Please." She whispered the word through dry lips. "Oh, please!"

"You will burn in the sun," he said, his eyes raking her

contours. "White skin is like the petal of a flower that browns and wrinkles in the heat. You must put on your dress."

Abruptly with the realisation that he spoke perfect English came the shock of realising that she was stark naked. An instant later she had ducked down to her neck again, her hands clasped across her breasts.

"You cannot stay there for the rest of your life," the man said, a ripple of amusement crossing his face.

"You speak English," Deborah said feebly.

"My mother was Irish, kidnapped from an emigrant train by the Navajos. You have heard of the Navajos?"

"Cousins to the Apaches," she said shiveringly.

"But with different customs." He displayed white teeth in a sardonic grin. "We Navajos don't take scalps."

Involuntarily she clutched at her mane of hair and his grin grew wider. "We have a great appreciation of female beauty," he added, "especially when it is unadorned, but you had better put on your dress."

"Not until you turn your back." Her fear ebbing now that it seemed she was not to be scalped at once, she stuck out her chin defiantly.

"Very well." He allowed himself another long, measuring look and then turned to gaze with apparently fascinated interest at the smooth face of the rock.

Deborah scrambled out of the pool and grabbed for her shift and drawers. She would have liked to stretch out and dry herself, but she was afraid that the stranger might turn round again, so she struggled into her undergarments and pulled on her dress, lacing it with trembling fingers.

"May I look now?" he enquired.

"If you like." She sat down and began to roll on her stockings.

"Do you have a name?" he asked, sitting down beside her and laying the rifle on the bank.

"Deborah. Deborah Jones. People call me Debbie."

"And you are with those people in the wagon up there?"

"You've seen them?" She gave him a startled look.

"For the last couple of days."

"But I didn't see you," she said.

"I would be a very poor tracker if you had been aware of me," he said, smiling again.

"Is that what you do? Track people?"

"Among other things. I am a man of two worlds and move between them according to need."

"Do you have a name?" she was emboldened to enquire.

"My mother named me Adam. That is my name in the white world. To my Indian relatives I am Leap-Over-The-Mountain."

"That's a strange name."

"I am called it because I travel much up and down the land. I lived with my mother's people for five years, learning to read and write and eat with knife and fork, but my heart is Navajo, so I came home to the hills again."

"I am from England," she confided. "My parents came over when I was ten years old, but they died three years ago of an influenza epidemic, and the Laycocks took me in."

"Why do you wear such ugly clothes?" he enquired, flicking the edge of her collar with a lean brown forefinger.

"They look quite pretty usually," she said defensively, "but we've been travelling for two months. Anyway, Mrs. Laycock says that vanity is a sin."

"You look more pretty without any clothes on," he observed. "When I saw you I thought I would like to make love to you. Even now, in that ugly dress, I would like to make love to you."

"That's a shocking thing to say!" she exclaimed, crimson flooding her face.

"Not shocking but very natural. I haven't had a woman for more than a month. That's a long time for a healthy man."

He was laughing at her again, but at the back of his eyes something leaped and shone, and there was a queer sick feeling in the pit of Deborah's stomach. She sat very still, looking at him, wanting him to touch her and fearing that he might, but he only shook his head slightly, saying, "Put on

your boots and we'll go back to the wagon. Your – Mr.
Laycock, was it? – won't shoot on sight?"

"He won't even shoot when he knows you well," Deborah
said, one of her irrepressible gusts of humour bubbling up in
her.

The sound of snores greeted them as they approached the
recumbent figures stretched in the shade. Then Jed leapt up,
yelling in consternation and fumbling for his rifle, and Mr.
Laycock thrust aside the hat that shaded his face and leaned
up on his elbow.

"This is Adam-Leap-The-Mountain," Deborah said hastily. "He's a tracker."

"Be thee harmed, Debbie?" Mrs. Laycock asked shiveringly.

"No, I'm quite all right." Deborah gave a small reassuring
smile.

"The young lady was washing in the pool when I made
myself known to her," Adam said.

"Thee speaks English, sir?" Mr. Laycock was on his feet
and shaking hands cordially, relief in his expression.

"My mother was white. I live here from choice, not neces-
sity," Adam said.

"John Laycock, sir, at thy service. This be my wife, Sarah,
and my daughter, Charity. Jed Williams is servant and
friend, and Deborah Jones there my ward."

"Thee will take coffee and a fresh baked scone, sir?" Mrs.
Laycock asked.

"With pleasure, ma'am." Adam lowered himself in one
graceful movement to the ground. "You can tell your man
he's no need to carry on pointing the rifle at me. I came alone
and intend no harm."

"Ain't never trusted a half-breed yet," Jed stated flatly.

"Put up thy weapon. Thee neglects the rules of courtesy,"
Mr. Laycock ordered.

"You're Quakers, from your turn of phrase." Adam
accepted a mug of coffee and bit into a scone.

"Members of the Society of Friends, sir, as thee says."

"Except for me. I'm a member of nothing, and I ain't very friendly," Jed said, chuckling dourly at his own wit.

"Where are you bound?" Adam, ignoring him, addressed the question to Mr. Laycock.

"Where the Lord bids, sir. I carry His Word to the Utes."

"The Utes! You pick a fierce tribe. They collect white scalps with as much pleasure as you might collect butterflies!"

"They be still children of the Lord," Mrs. Laycock said, "and entitled to hear of God."

"They've heard of Him, though to them He has a different name," Adam said. "You'd be wiser to contact the Pueblos if you've a mind to make converts. They're a gentle people, half of them Catholics already, settled in villages and hospitable to strangers."

"Then they have little need of our help," Mr. Laycock said.

"But you take your family into very grave danger," Adam argued. "Have you no thought for your wife and daughter?"

"No sense in wasting your breath," Jed announced, lowering his rifle and regarding Adam with something like approval. "He'll simply tell you the Lord is leading us."

"He has led us thus far without hurt," Mrs. Laycock said mildly. "All the way from Kansas City in two months."

"Along a well-marked trail in a green summer," Adam said, his voice edged with impatience. "You've left the grasslands behind you now, sir, and you've four hundred miles of mountain range to cross. With the best will in the world you'll not make more than ten miles a day – less, if we have a cold spell. That'll bring you to the end of October, with the winter ahead and your supplies just about finished."

"What ought we to do?" Deborah asked. It was bad manners to interrupt one's elders, but what he was saying matched her own fears.

"Turn south and winter at Santa Fe," he said promptly. "You can go westward again when the spring comes."

"And leave a pagan people without the Word for all the

winter? Thee means kindly, sir, but we cannot heed thee."

"Are there houses at Santa Fe?" Charity asked, her round face wistful.

"Houses of brick and stone," Adam assured her. "Plenty of beef and grain in the stockyards and warehouses."

"It would be pleasant," she said, glancing at her father.

"Child, cannot thee understand that this is a temptation, and a subtle one?" Mr. Laycock said reprovingly. "The Devil wears a fair face sometimes – I mean no disrespect to you, sir, for I am certain thee means well. But we cannot turn aside now."

"Then you will run your family into danger because of your stubbornness," Adam said bluntly.

"Where there is Faith there is no real danger," the other said serenely.

"Then I'll not try to persuade you further," Adam said, rising. "You'd do well to make as fast a speed as you can while the weather holds. Has your guide here staked out the trail before?"

"I've been as far as Virgin," Jed said, "but I reckon I can point my nose due west and get everybody else there with me."

"I wish you good fortune," Adam said, his expression more sombre than hopeful.

"Thee's welcome to ride along with us for a time," Mr. Laycock offered.

"My thanks, but my horse is tethered beyond the bluff. I've a report to make and ride faster alone."

"A report? To whom?" Jed asked, suspicion in his face again.

"To my people. There is talk of troop movements in the area. We keep our eyes open."

"Are thy people on the warpath, then?" Mrs. Laycock enquired nervously. "We were told the Navajos were to be resettled peaceably."

"The fool who commands Fort Wingate ordered us to Bosque Redondo reservation in July," Adam nodded. "The

Army destroyed our grain and drove off our cattle in an effort to persuade us, but we have no intention of being penned up at the whim of the Government."

"Then thee will break the Treaty?" Mr. Laycock frowned.

"The Treaty was broken two years ago, and not by us," Adam said. "Half a dozen youngsters got liquored up on firewater and went on a cattle-stealing foray. The Tribal Council would have dealt with them, but Carleton decided that a massacre would serve his purpose."

"We heard of that. It was a shocking thing," Mrs. Laycock said.

"Carleton was commended for his firm and prompt action against the renegades," Adam said wryly. "Renegades! Three of the dead were not five years old, and half of them were women. It was cold-blooded murder."

"There have been wrongs on both sides," Mr. Laycock said.

"And more to follow, unless the Government changes its policy and leaves us in peace. As it is, Manuelito, our chief, intends to ask for a new treaty. We will give safe conduct to whites passing through our lands if we are left alone in our own country. God knows there's room for all."

"Thee is a Christian, sir?" Mrs. Laycock said hopefully.

"Catholic on my mother's side and a follower of the Great White Spirit on my father's side," he grinned.

"Perhaps there is need for us among the Navajos, my dear?" She looked enquiringly at her husband.

"I have set my heart on a mission to the Utes," he said obstinately.

"And I go to inform my relatives that you are one small family of emigrants, not worth the trouble of raiding. I bid you goodbye, ma'am. Mr. Laycock, sir."

He was going and Deborah felt a stab of disappointment, for he hadn't even glanced in her direction. But as he strode across the sunburned grass he turned his head briefly to call, "Don't leave the dishes you were washing behind, Miss Debbie."

"I'll get them now!" She sprang up and ran across to the narrow path between the rocks. The plates and mugs were still scattered on the bank, and she knelt to gather them up.

"Miss Debbie," Adam had paused and was looking down at her, his voice low. "Do you mean to continue your journey? It will be a harsh one with nothing but danger at the end."

"I've no choice," she said. "The Laycock's have been good to me."

"But they're not blood-kin?"

"No, but when my parents died – they were neighbours, you see, but my father left only debts. Mr. Laycock paid them all and took me in."

"If you rode with me now I'd take you to Santa Fe. You could find work there, and you'd be safe. Don't you want to live to be old? You'll not do it among the Utes."

"I cannot," she said, crushing down temptation. "It would be ungrateful."

"Plenty of loyalty, but no sense." He leaned down, put his hands on her shoulders and drew her up to face him. "Do you know how to fire a rifle?"

Deborah shook her head.

"Make the man Jed show you the way," he advised. "If you're attacked, shoot to kill."

"It is forbidden—"

"Mr. Laycock will be too busy praying to scold you. Shoot to kill," he repeated.

"But I don't have any guns. Only Jed and Mr. Laycock carry rifles for the killing of game."

"Do you have a knife?"

"Only a little pen-knife, and it isn't very sharp."

"Take this, then." He passed a narrow leather sheath into her hands. "Keep it hidden."

"But I don't think I could bring myself to kill anyone," she protested.

"If you're taken by the Utes, use it on yourself," he said.

"It's a quicker death than the one they'll give you. Remember."

He drew his hand down the side of her face in a tender, protective gesture, turned and went, leaping from rock to rock as agilely as a goat, and then vanishing from sight.

Deborah turned the leather sheath over in her hands. There was a pattern of red and yellow interlocking squares on it. Slowly she drew out the narrow, wickedly sharp little knife and shivered, wondering if she would ever find the courage to pierce her own flesh. It was a terrible sin to take one's own life, but it would be even more terrible to be taken alive by the Utes.

"Debbie, is thee coming back?" Mrs. Laycock was picking her way down to the stream. Hastily Deborah pushed the knife back into the sheath, concealing it in the folds of her skirt.

"He was a fine-looking man, was he not?" The older woman was looking at her with a mixture of affection and regret.

"I never saw a half-breed before," Deborah said.

"We will probably see many such. Some people don't trust them, but 'tis my belief many of them combine the best of both races. Come, child, we must pack these away. John wishes to make more distance before sunset."

"Are you afraid of the Utes?" Deborah asked curiously.

"Child, sometimes I am afraid of everything," Mrs. Laycock said, weariness in her face. "But we learn to live with fear, and so conquer it. Thee and Charity are young and have not yet affirmed the Word, but that will come in its own time."

"You could tell him to go south for the winter. He might listen to you," Deborah said earnestly.

"See this ring, Debbie." Mrs. Laycock held out her hand to show the broad gold band on her finger. "John had it engraved with our initials and a heart between them. I promised to obey and honour him, and that means to follow him wherever the Lord bids him travel. Thee will understand when thee meets a man fit for the marrying."

"Out in the desert? Will there be any husbands there?"

"There will be a settlement somewhere. Many are coming out to the west," Mrs. Laycock said. "Fine young men with courage and ambition, who will wish to settle and take a good wife. And thee is young still."

"Eighteen. I shall be an old maid in a couple of years," Deborah replied.

"Then thee must be a good one," Mrs. Laycock said.

"Yes." Deborah stifled a sigh as she picked up the remaining dishes. The sheath-knife in her hand was both a promise and a threat. She couldn't resist another glance at the high cliff where Adam-Leap-The-Mountain had been poised briefly before he had disappeared from view. It was unlikely that she would ever see him again, but she hugged the hope of it to herself as she followed Mrs. Laycock back to the wagon.

CHAPTER
TWO

IN the days that followed, the image of that tall, copper skinned, buckskin-clad figure floated gently behind Deborah's closed eyelids when she lay down to sleep at night, and by day as they trekked slowly over the high plateau she could fancy, if she screwed up her eyes slightly, that she saw him, striding ahead with his rifle hanging loosely from his hand. But when she opened her eyes wide only Jed Williams with his scraggy beard and homespun breeches, or Mr. Laycock in his shabby black suit and low-crowned hat was there.

They were still making good time, the six patient oxen pulling the heavy, iron-rimmed wagon for mile after mile across ground covered with scrub grass and pierced with the scarlet blossoms of the cactus flower. On the slopes were occasional fir trees, their spindly outlines contrasting with the thick, greyish-green lichen that covered the lower rocks and boulders. The water-holes were fewer now, the wind keener, and on the far peaks was already a thin white edging of snow.

Charity had exclaimed how pretty they looked and received a frowning shake of the head from Jed. "Let that snowline get lower, blocking the passes, and we'll end up like the Donner party," he warned.

"What was the Donner party?" she wanted to know.

"A packet of fools who took a short cut to California and were cut off by snow in the High Sierras."

"Did they die?"

"Not all of them, Missy. Them as did got eaten by the others, and when spring came them as was left had the taste for human flesh. There's some say as it never left them."

"Has thee nothing better to do than fill maids' heads with horror tales?" Mrs. Laycock scolded.

"Is it true?" Charity's blue eyes were wide with fear. "Did they really—?"

"I believe something of the sort did occur, dear, but for myself I always thought that the story must have been grossly exaggerated," her mother consoled. "After all, we are human beings, not vultures or hyenas!"

"If we get snowed in," Deborah said, "I'll make certain that Jed provides the first course!"

The others shuddered and laughed, and then Mr. Laycock called them to evening prayers, but Jed's words lingered uneasily in Deborah's mind. Was it possible that, driven by extremes, human beings could become no better than animals? It was hard to realise as they sat round the fire of oxen chips and brushwood that such things might be. That night she dreamed and woke, not remembering what the dream had been about but filled with formless apprehension, and lay, shivering in her thick blanket, listening to the howl of a coyote somewhere beyond the clearing where they had pitched camp for the night.

The going was rougher now, great boulders flung by some careless celestial hand often blocking their way, darkness falling like a black shroud over the landscape.

"Time to get some supplies in, Mr. Laycock," Jed announced when they stopped one midday for the first of the two daily meals.

"My flour stocks are very low," Mrs. Laycock said hopefully.

"Fresh meat's all I can provide, ma'am. There are no trading posts hereabouts," Jed grinned. "But with any luck we'll get some tasty buckrabbit – even a deer, if I can go down into one of the valleys."

"How long will you be gone?" Deborah asked.

"Set off now, get in some shooting before dark, bed down

overnight, couple of hours' shooting, back here – by tomorrow afternoon!"

"Then we shall wait here for thee," Mr. Laycock said. "'Tis a pleasant spot."

"It'll mean the loss of a day's journeying," Mrs. Laycock said, looking concerned.

"To rest the animals, Sarah, and afford thee time to bake and wash," her husband reminded her. "We will have a prayer meeting too, so that the Lord may know we are still mindful of Him. We could begin with that if thee has a mind, Jed."

"When I get back I'll do plenty of praying," Jed said hastily, "but I'm thinking it'll make good sense for me to get moving as soon as I can. Quicker I start, sooner I get back."

"Thee will take care, Jed?" Mrs. Laycock said anxiously. "We think highly of thee."

"I'll be back." Jed, looking slightly embarrassed as he always did when praised, whistled between his teeth as he stumped off towards the sturdy little cob pony on which he and Mr. Laycock took turns in riding.

"We must make good use of the hours ahead," Mrs. Laycock said briskly. "I've the wagon to clean and the bread to bake and the clothes to be washed."

"We'll wash the clothes," Deborah said promptly. "Charity and I can do them while you clear the wagon and get your bread made."

"Thee cannot wash dirty garments at a drinking pool," Mrs. Laycock objected.

"We'll take them down to the river, then. We saw it over to the right as we crested the ridge."

"Child, 'tis more than a mile away and out of sight of the wagon!"

"And we can be there and back within two hours. There's nothing for miles and miles, so what possible harm could come to us?" Deborah argued.

"John, what is thy word on this?" Mrs. Laycock turned to her husband.

"I warrant they'll be safe enough," he said consideringly. "They're no longer children, and we do wrong to keep them close penned."

"If they were to get lost—" she trembled.

"Sarah, use thy sense," he rebuked. "The path to the river leads almost straight from the bluff. A blind man could find his way."

"Animals—"

"Are not likely to attack in the open, in the heat of the day. But if 'twill ease thy mind I'll give Debbie the rifle."

"She cannot use it."

"Yes, I can," Debbie said eagerly. "Jed showed me the other day how to load and fire it."

"If thee meets danger, fire one shot into the air," he instructed. "Aim into the sky now."

"Yes, of course." She took the rifle gratefully, pleased by the confidence he reposed in her.

"The Lord go with thee. We will have prayer meeting when thee returns," he said.

"And clean clothes," Charity said, staggering down from the wagon with two large bundles.

"Give me one of them," Deborah ordered, "and put your sunbonnet straight or you'll get fever."

"Thee sounds like me!" Mrs. Laycock said, smiling.

"If they follow thy example, my love, both of them will be fine women," Mr. Laycock said, putting his arm round his wife's shoulders. "Be careful of the rifle, Debbie. One shot in the air if thee be alarmed."

"I'll remember." She smiled at them both and set off as briskly as her burden would allow, with Charity following in her wake.

The path down to the river twisted between overhanging rocks and emerged on a stony plateau at the far side of which the river ran threadlike between low banks of red sandstone. The sun shimmered along the ground, sending up waves of heat that made it seem more like high summer than the end of autumn.

Distances were deceptive in this wild landscape. By the time they reached the edge of the river Deborah's arms and legs were aching, and even Charity's bright chatter had dwindled to an occasional remark.

"Mother put in a bar of soap. She has only six left." The girl dropped her bundle and bent to untie it. "I wonder what we'll do when all the soap and the food has gone."

"There'll be a settlement at Virgin. We can get supplies there," Deborah said.

"Will there really be other white people out in the desert?" the younger girl asked.

"There are bound to be. Your father wouldn't take us all there if nobody else had ever been," Deborah said, vigorously swishing a garment in the swift-flowing water. It ran icy cold over her hands and forearms, and the sun, beating down on her head, competed with a keen wind that spiralled down from the heights, bringing with it the scent of snow.

"Perhaps the Utes killed them, or they all ate one another," Charity said.

"Thee should have more faith," Deborah said in a very creditable imitation of Mr. Laycock's deep, mild tones.

"I don't think I shall ever have such a whole-hearted belief," Charity said, her rosy face suddenly serious. "Will you publicly affirm when the time comes?"

"I don't know." Deborah considered for a moment and then said teasingly, "If the people have all eaten one another up there won't be many to hear! We'd better lay these things flat in order to dry them."

"I'll get some stones to hold them down," Charity offered, hunting around for some flat ones that she could lift.

"And we'll have a rest in the shade before we start back." Deborah straightened from her task and looked about, wondering where they might find a cool spot.

"Those cliffs over there might have caves," the younger girl suggested.

"We'll fill the water-bottles and have a look." Suiting action to words, Deborah plunged the leather flask into the swirling water, brought it out dripping, and stoppered it carefully.

The cliffs rose sheer into the sky, but as they approached them narrow clefts and fissures came into view, some tunnelling into the rock face and widening into caves. Charity darted ahead, twisting herself into one of the inlets. Her voice, distorted by echoes floated back. "Debbie, do come and see. It's quite a big cave inside and there are pictures on the walls!"

"What sort of pictures?" Deborah bent under an overhanging shelf of rock into a cool, dim interior.

"Animals, and men killing them with spears and bows and arrows." Charity was pointing eagerly.

In the greenish light the deeply scratched figures had a mysterious, lifelike quality. The red and yellow ochre with which they had once been smeared was fading slightly now, but the outlines were sharp. "I wonder who made them," Charity mused.

"People who lived here hundreds of years ago, I suppose." Deborah peered at them. "I think they were meant as a kind of magic. A hunter made a picture of himself killing an animal, and then he believed the real killing would happen."

"Then I shall make a picture of me living in a house and wearing a dress with hoops!" Charity glanced around the floor of the cave then selecting a piece of yellowish stone from the foot of the rock wall, she set to work on an undecorated space.

"Your father says hooped skirts are a foolish vanity," Deborah observed, sitting down and tucking her own modest skirts beneath her.

"I'd still like one." Charity was drawing busily. "What would you like, Debbie, if you could draw a picture that would really come true?"

A tall figure in buckskins with a fierce hawk face and hands that held her tightly, dissolving her flesh to water. "It's very wicked to pay heed to superstition," she said aloud. "Your parents would be very upset."

"It's only a game!" Charity pouted.

"Well, it's a very silly one," Deborah said firmly, "and it's time we were getting back. We can finish drying off the clothes up on the ridge. What was that?"

"What was what? I didn't hear anything."

"I did – a kind of drumming. Listen! It's getting louder."

"Perhaps its rain or thunder."

They stood in silence, their expressions tense.

"I hear it now," Charity whispered. "It's coming from outside."

"Stay here. I'm going to take a look." Picking up the rifle, Deborah went to the narrow entrance and peeped cautiously out. The plateau, with its tumbled rocks and swift ribbon of river met her gaze, but the drumming was clear, vibrating from one end of the empty space to the other.

"Debbie, what *is* it?" Charity was tugging at her sleeve.

"Drums. Indian drums. I never heard them before."

"They send messages like that, don't they?" Charity whispered. "I wonder what they're saying."

"I don't know, but I think we ought to stay here for a while." Deborah frowned, trying to think what best to do. "They may have seen the wagon up on the high ground and be telling one another we are harmless, but we'll wait a while."

"It sounds creepy," Charity said nervously.

"That's only because we don't understand it," Deborah said stoutly. "For all we know it may be someone's birthday and they're sending greetings."

But the insistent rhythm had a sinister quality that grated on her nerves. It went on and on, rising to a crescendo, dying to a heartbeat. And then suddenly there was silence.

"Have they gone?" Charity asked. Her words were drowned in a succession of yells and screams that seemed to come from directly above their heads. Deborah, glancing up, had a flashing vision of unshod hoofs and bare brown legs, before she flung herself down behind the concealing rock, pulling Charity with her. The screams were diminishing into the distance, but the drums had started up again, beating relentlessly through the still air, and as she cautiously raised her head again flames sprang up on the high ridge where the wagon was camped.

"Debbie, what's happening? What's going on?" Charity was struggling to her feet, alarm on her face.

"They're attacking the wagon," Deborah said, her voice tense.

"Attacking it! But my parents mean no harm to anyone. They're not even armed!"

"Get back into the cave!" Deborah pushed the younger girl down the narrow passage.

"Can't you fire the rifle?" Charity begged.

"There's only one shot in it! It wouldn't do any good," Debbie said.

"But we can't just leave them!" Charity sobbed. "What about Jed? Will he have heard them and turned back? Debbie, oh Debbie! What are we going to do?"

Deborah shook her violently, her own face contorted. "Be quiet, or you'll have the Utes down on to us too," she said harshly. "Do you want to be scalped as well?"

"Perhaps they escaped?" Charity's blue eyes pleaded for comfort.

"There must be about a hundred Indians," Deborah said, "and there's no place for them to run or hide."

"Jed—?"

"Will have been taken already. You'd best make up your mind to it. They're all dead and the wagon is burning, and we daren't go back to make certain or we'll be captured too!"

Charity gave one horrified look and burst into tears of fright and grief. Deborah's own eyes were dry, her mind racing as if the sudden turn of events had speeded her thoughts. It had all happened so quickly, the mounted figures seeming to rise up out of nothing and the drums sounding like the echoes of ghostly thunder. She had no doubt that the Laycocks were dead. She hoped indeed that they were dead, and not held for torture by the savages. At all events they couldn't risk going back to the wagon to find out. Nor could they stay where they were for very long. Before sunset the Utes would probably come down to the river to water their horses, and seeing the clothes drying on the bank might take it into their heads to search the neighbouring caves. She and Charity would have to move out, trusting that the Indians would be too busy firing the wagon to have time to notice stragglers.

The girl's weeping had subsided and she looked dazed, as if she were in a dream from which there would be no waking. Deborah spoke firmly, thrusting her own fear to the back of her mind.

"Charity, we can't stay here lest the Utes come and find us. We'll have to move out now, following the line of the river and keeping in the shade. We've plenty of water and I've got the rifle."

"With one shot in it," Charity gulped.

"Never mind. We'll save it for a nice fat deer. Come now, and walk close behind me."

She gave the other a brief hug, and went forward steadily until they were at the rock face again. The Indians were too far away now for their yells to be heard, but flames danced on the skyline from the burning wagon.

They edged along in the shade of the high cliffs, moving further from the high ridge. If the Utes had posted a guard he would have spotted them in a moment, but it was evident they hadn't considered it necessary, for the two girls went unchallenged. A steep gully winding between river and rocks took them out of the plateau into a series of narrow hills and valleys with no definite trail, but plenty of concealment from scrubgrass and boulders.

"Which way are we going?" Charity asked in bewilderment.

Deborah stared round, biting her lip. They were certainly moving away from the burning wagon, but she had no means of knowing where the Utes were camped. They had seemed to spring up from every direction at once. Even the river had trickled into a narrow stream, emptying itself over the rocks into a weed-fringed pool. Ahead of them the landscape was folded into deep crevices, and their shadows were growing longer in the setting sun.

"We'll go to the west," she said at last, making her voice brightly confident. "There's a settlement at Virgin, you know."

"How far away is it?" Charity was beginning to take an interest in her surroundings, but her questions were awkward ones.

"As far as it takes to walk," Deborah said. "We can make ten or fifteen miles a day if we take it steadily."

"Without any food?"

"We've plenty of water." Deborah's voice quavered only slightly. "There are lots of things to eat in the high country. Fish in the streams, and berries and edible roots, and prickly pear, oh, lots of things! The Indians manage, don't they? And mountain men live up here all the year round. We'll get by."

Her assumption of confidence evidently satisfied the girl, for she rubbed her tear-stained cheeks and managed a watery smile.

They walked on, skirting boulders, scrambling up little paths that brought them to higher ridges with more reaching up into the distance. The wind stung their ears and noses, and the sun was a dull red disc in a grieving sky.

"We'll make camp now," Deborah said at last. "We'll have a swallow of water each and pack moss round us to keep off the cold. Then we can start off again at first light. We'll walk for three hours and rest for an hour until sunset comes. We'll probably be able to catch a fish in one of the streams."

How she would contrive it was, fortunately, a question that Charity didn't ask. Shock and grief had taken its toll of her and she lay down obediently, allowing herself to be covered with the thick moss that Deborah pulled from the surrounding rocks. If she cried herself silently to sleep

Deborah was not aware of it, for she herself fell at once into the blackness of deep slumber.

A cold, grey dawn with no gleam of sun waked her. She wriggled out of the cavern of moss and washed her face, catching the splashing water in her cupped hands. There were berries growing in profusion on low bushes further down the ravine. She picked as many as her apron would hold and took them back to Charity, who was stirring.

"My parents—" The girl's voice trailed away miserably as memory flooded back.

"It does no good to think of them," Deborah said firmly. "Eat the berries now. I found two biscuits in my pocket, so we'll have half of one now and keep the other for tomorrow."

"Couldn't we go back, just in case?" Charity began.

"It's better that we don't," Deborah said. "Better that we remember them as they were. Eat your breakfast now, and this evening we'll catch a big fish."

Charity had apparently accepted her authority without question, for she meekly chewed her biscuit and berries and went, without being told, to wash her face and comb her hair.

They set off again, moving away from the rising sun, walking as briskly as they could over the rough ground. Now and then Deborah paused, straining her ears for drums or hoofbeats, but there was nothing except the singing of the wind and the cry of some unidentified bird over their heads. They were apparently the only human beings in a land of scrub and rock and little trickling streams.

By mid-afternoon Deborah was so hungry that she could imagine her stomach cleaving to her backbone. It was fortunate, she thought wryly, that both she and Charity had grown accustomed to walking, because at least they were not likely to become exhausted too soon. What did worry her was the increasing cold. Their dresses and sunbonnets were little protection against the biting wind that blew more strongly as they moved further into the passes. With growing uneasiness she noticed the frost-rimed grass.

Her boast of providing fish for supper was as empty as she feared it would be. Anything she managed to catch would have to be dying of old age, she thought ruefully. Instead they finished off the remaining berries and lay down hungry, pulling what bracken they could find over themselves.

The cold was piercing. Two or three times she woke with freezing hands and feet, to hear Charity whimpering in her sleep. The girl was harder to rouse in the morning, and she sat shivering and weeping while Deborah rubbed her chilled limbs and carefully divided the remaining biscuit.

"Are you sure we're going the right way?" she asked tearfully.

"Absolutely certain," Deborah lied. "We must have come near twenty miles already, and we'll make good time again today."

"But we've nothing left to eat."

"I've got the rifle. We'll bring down a deer or a rabbit later on and have a big supper, but right now we have to get moving again!"

Deborah yanked her companion to her feet, chafing her hands bracingly. As they trudged on she found herself repeating silently over and over, "I won't waste the shot. I won't waste the shot."

That the noise might alert any Utes in the vicinity was a possibility she dared not consider. If the worst happened she still had the knife that Adam Leap-The-Mountain had given to her, and she would use it on Charity and herself.

The rabbit appeared quite suddenly as they stretched out their legs in a rest period. It was destined for its first and last encounter with the human race, for as it sat up to wash its ears Deborah saw it, took aim and fired before she was consciously aware of having done so. The echoes reverberated round the narrow canyon where they were sheltering, but the animal fell, twitched for a moment, and was still.

"You really can shoot!" Charity exclaimed.

"A fluke," Deborah said, modestly and truthfully. "You start off a fire on that rock over there and I'll get it skinned."

It took ages to get even a small fire going and the rabbit was not as well-fed as she had hoped, but it tasted marvellous. They ate the charred meat in their fingers, savouring its sweetness, and the skin, scraped clean with the knife, provided a muff for Charity's numbed hands. They even risked leaving the little pile of twigs and grass to burn itself out, for the dancing flames gave an illusion of warmth.

But morning brought the first flurry of snow, whirling into their faces and dropping cold on to their feet and fingers. It was no more than a flurry, gone as quickly as it had arisen, but it laid the threat of winter like an icy finger across Deborah's heart.

"We'll keep to the lower passes today," she said briskly, wrapping the skin firmly round Charity's hands. "I reckon we'll cover plenty of ground if we cut down the rest periods."

Charity made no answer but went on staring past Deborah with eyes and mouth open. From her throat came a little gurgling sound.

"Charity?" Slowly Deborah turned, her own eyes widening as she saw the two mounted Indians who sat their ponies at a few yards' distance and regarded them unblinkingly.

"Utes?" Charity whispered. "Are they Utes?"

"I don't know." Deborah's own throat was closing in terror. "I don't know."

"What are we going to do?" the younger girl said. "Debbie, what are we going to do?"

"We'll walk forward," Deborah said, "and we'll sing."

"Sing?" Charity's voice squeaked.

"Sing very loudly." Someone else seemed to be using her mind and lips, for she heard her own words with a sense of utter disbelief. "We'll sing 'Christmas is Coming'. Very loud. You remember it!"

She was not certain if she remembered the words herself, but her legs were carrying her forward over the rocky ground and her voice, thin and tuneless, rose into the snow-whitened air.

"Christmas is coming,
The goose is getting fat,
Please put a penny—"

The Indians were conferring together. She heard a language that sounded like spitting and then the taller of the two, his expression still blank, tossed down a bundle that had been slung over the back of his pony.

"I'm going to faint," Charity said in a high voice that trembled on the edge of a scream.

"If you do I'll leave you here," Deborah said, and went on singing, her voice gaining strength, though she couldn't have told what words came out.

The one who had flung down the bundle was tapping the side of his head. The other said something sharply to him and they wheeled their ponies about and galloped off, crouched low over the flowing manes.

"What happened? Why didn't they kill us?" Forgetting her promise to faint, Charity tugged impatiently at Deborah.

"They thought we were crazy, out of our minds," Deborah said. She was in a state between laughing and crying, but laughter won and she held her sides, giggling with the tears drying on her lashes. "Jed told me once that the Indians fear crazy people and treat them with respect because they believe they have powers not given to ordinary folk! They thought we were crazy!"

"They left the bundle for us." Charity ran towards it.

"Two buffalo hides." Deborah fumbled at the folded and tied package. "I think it's one hide cut in half, but they'll keep us warm."

"Fish!" Charity's voice was ecstatic. "Two big smoked fish, and some flat cakes, and – what's this?"

"Jerky. Dried buffalo meat. You soak it in water and then eat it. Jed told me. I hope they didn't give us all their supplies."

"This will last a long time, won't it?" Charity's blue eyes begged for reassurance.

"Days, and then some!" Deborah seized one of the hides and wrapped it about her companion.

"And by then we might be at Virgin?"

Down the gully the wind eddied and mocked and the sun retreated before a bank of white cloud, but Deborah's voice was brimful of confidence.

"I promise you," she said gaily.

CHAPTER
THREE

"WE'RE not going to get anywhere, are we?"

Charity's voice had a hopeless ring. A week had passed since their encounter with the Indians, or perhaps it had been longer. Deborah was beginning to lose count of the nights they had huddled together in windswept gullies, or the days of trudging over the high ranges with the rocks carved into cathedrals by the ceaseless wind and the streams half frozen. They had eaten the last of the bread that morning, soaking it in a puddle to soften it. Now there was only one piece of the leathery jerky and one bottle of water left, and ahead of them the landscape stretched in unending hostility.

"We'll get there." She made her voice strong and gay. "It's a miracle we've come so far already, and miracles don't just stop in the middle. We'll get there, you'll see!"

Brave words, she thought ruefully, when they stopped to rest. And they meant precisely nothing at all, because the truth was that she had no clear idea where they were headed. In this country it would be possible to pass by a camp settled in the next ridge and never even know it was there. Soon, as they grew weaker from lack of food, the vultures would begin to circle. In her imagination she could already feel a tearing at her flesh.

She must have drifted into a half-sleep, in which though she was conscious of leaning against the sloping stone with the buffalo hide wrapped round her she also seemed to be in some other place, cradled in strong arms with a voice whispering to her words that fled almost before they were spoken.

This way lay madness! She opened her eyes and shook her head vigorously to clear it. A few yards away, silhouett against the white sky, a line of mounted figures stared back at her, faces impassive under topknots wound round with red cloth. They were clad warmly in buckskins and heavy jackets of buffalo and leather, and there were bows and arrows slung across the manes of their ponies.

"Navajo?" She put out a restraining hand towards Charity who was scrambling to her feet. "Are you Navajo?"

For a heart-stopping instant there was no reply. Then one of them, taller than the rest, dismounted and walked towards her, speaking in careful English.

"You are woman who belongs to Adam Leap-The-Mountain? He tell us seek for woman with red hair."

"Yes. Yes, I am." At that moment she would have claimed to be anybody's property.

The Indian put out his hand and jerked her to her feet, pushing back the buffalo robe and the crumpled linen bonnet. Her hair, glowing about her white face, sprang up in a tangle of curls.

"You ride with us. Not very far." He called something over his shoulder to the others and they came down the rise, another dismounting to pull Charity upright. Deborah found herself lifted astride a pony saddled only with a blanket, and then the man who had spoken leapt up behind her, and they were riding hard across the half-frozen ground into the biting wind.

Darkness was falling when they stopped and she was dimly aware of being lifted down and wrapped up in extra skins. The snow was thicker on the ground here, but the men were clearing a circle and building a fire. She watched them, fear and fatigue giving place to curiosity, as they murmured among themselves in a language that sometimes sounded like Spanish and sometimes like nothing she had ever heard before. The flames sprang up cheerfully and the scent of roasting meat drifted to her nostrils. At a little distance a young brave was cutting chunks of bread off a flat loaf with a gleaming knife and passing them round.

The man with whom she had ridden broke off a piece of

crisped meat and gave it to her, his voice abrupt but not unfriendly.

"Eat well. Sleep well. We ride again soon."

The meat was deer, she guessed, but she was so hungry she would have swallowed anything. Cramming it into her mouth she saw him shake his head, his tone chiding. "Slow," he said. "Eat slow. Eat quick, get sick." His expression was so much like that of an anxious nursemaid that she wanted to laugh. From the other side of the fire Charity called sleepily, "Is it all right to eat it?"

"Yes, of course. We're safe now." Deborah spoke loudly, hoping that it was true. "Eat slowly and then get some sleep. I don't know how far we have to go, but it won't take us long."

"Did the half-breed we met send them?" Charity asked.

"I suppose so." Deborah swallowed the last of her meat and raised her voice, speaking slowly and distinctly. "Is Adam Leap-The-Mountain your chief?"

"Chief?" The man stared at her for a moment, then shook his head. "No. Not chief. Manuelito is our chief. Adam is scout."

"I see. Thank you." She would have liked to ask more questions, but he had turned away and was wrapping himself in his coverings.

At dawn, with flakes of snow drifting from a sunless sky, she was shaken awake and pulled to her feet where she swayed dizzily for a moment. The Indian was pointing to a place behind the rocks, his gestures indicating that she and Charity could make a private toilet.

The younger girl looked brighter and more cheerful after the food and sleep, but her face was filthy, her lips chapped with cold, her long yellow plaits matted. One of the men, stepping forward as the girls returned to the clearing, took the end of one plait in a lean brown hand and said something in his own tongue to his companions. There was a burst of laughter as quickly stifled, and then they were lifted up to the ponies again and the journey continued in silence.

They were descending now, the bare stone giving place to scrubland and sagebrush. Here and there Deborah spotted cottonwood and juniper trees, their branches outlined delicately with snow. They were riding into a canyon, its walls high and smooth of a reddish colour muted now by a thin layer of ice. There were patches here, staked and planted, and against the sheltering stone fruit trees were ranged, their bare branches like skeleton fingers, their trunks packed with moss.

"Where are we? What is this place?" She twisted around to look into her companion's face.

"Canyon de Chelly. Big Navajo village," he returned. "We come to Adam Leap-The-Mountain soon."

"With my hair in rats' tails and my bones sticking through my flesh," Deborah thought. "He's likely to take one look and throw me out on to the plateau again."

She sat up as straight as she could, trying to ignore the ache in her back and legs. She could see houses now – huts of wood and stone set between the trees with smoke rising from low chimneys. There were people coming out to stare at them, women wrapped in heavy shawls with babies strapped in wicker cradles to their backs, two little boys with miniature bows and arrows who ran alongside the ponies, a grizzled old man with long moustaches and several bright feathers stuck through his red headband.

The canyon was widening into a clearing thick with grass tipped with frost, and more Indians were hurrying out, not talking or smiling, but watching out of dark, sloe-slanted eyes. Deborah was lifted down and stood, wondering what she was expected to do.

Then the door of one of the wooden huts scattered about the clearing opened and the tall, buckskin-clad figure whose features were etched on her memory, strode up to her.

"Adam!" His name rose joyfully to her lips and trailed away as she met his unsmiling gaze. There was not the faintest hint of welcome in his tone as he said,

"Deborah, come with me. The other can go with the women."

He had turned on his heel before she could answer and was walking back to the hut. From behind her Charity said crossly, "What does that mean? Where am I to be taken?"

"Go with them. I'll see you later," Deborah said impatiently. "They won't hurt you!"

Charity, giving a doubtful look at the elderly woman who had taken her arm, evidently thought better of arguing and went meekly.

From the doorway Adam called sharply, without turning round, "Deborah!"

Her pleasure at seeing him was drowned in indignation. How dare he speak to her as if she really were his property? Perhaps he had lived so long among savages that he had forgotten how to behave with a gentlewoman!

Ignoring the silent, clustering Indians she marched after him, tripping over the edge of the buffalo hide as she stepped into the room. There was a fire crackling in a central hearth with a pot suspended on a chain over it, and a mattress piled with blankets and furs running the length of one wall. Light came through slats in the barred windows and a lamp hung from the ceiling, and there were shelves along another wall. That much she took in, and then Adam kicked the door shut and faced her with outstretched hand.

"Thank God you made it!" he said briefly. "The Hopis brought word of two crazy white squaws trying to cross the high country. We thought you dead with the rest of your people."

"You knew about that?" She forgot her anger and stared at him.

"The Utes like to boast of their slaughters," he said. "One of the Hopis mentioned a woman with red hair, and I knew then that you had got away. I sent some of the youngsters out to bring you in."

"Kind of you to bother!" she said tartly. "You didn't think of riding out yourself, I suppose."

"Manuelito and some of the young bucks are away on a cattle raid, so I was needed here," he said calmly. "Take your things off. They can practically stand up by themselves, from the look of them."

"You could at least have said you were pleased to see me," she said in a small voice. "I don't like to be yelled at."

"It would be considered very bad manners to go hugging and kissing you in public," he said. "As for yelling at you – all Indians yell at their wives, in case they might be suspected of being henpecked."

"Oh, I see – *wives*!" She stared at him, her mouth open in dismay. "But I'm not your wife!"

"Not yet, but I told the others you were my woman. The ceremony will take place when Manuelito gets back with the cattle."

"*What* ceremony?" Deborah demanded.

"The wedding," he said. "Herrero Grande will perform the ceremony. He's the main chieftain of the Navajo."

"A savage to perform a wedding!"

"Herrero is a fine leader, well fitted to join two people together. We can go to Santa Fe later if you like, and have a priest tie the knot in Christian fashion."

"But I've no intention of marrying you," she said faintly.

"You mean you've seen someone you like better?" Adam stood back, grinning at her.

"I mean I don't intend to marry anybody," Deborah said firmly. "Now, if you'll excuse me, I'll go and join Charity with the women."

"Charity is quite safe where she is," Adam said calmly. "You are my woman and you stay here."

"Don't order me about!" Her green eyes snapped with temper.

"I'm simply telling you," he said patiently, "that you were brought here as my woman, and as such will enjoy a certain respect among other women. Do you really want me to tell them you're free for all comers?"

"You may tell them whatever you please," she retorted, "but nobody can force me to do anything against my will!"

"You will learn differently," he began, but she flung open the door and walked out, too annoyed to be amused at the scattering of those still thronging the clearing.

"Charity!" She raised her voice as she hitched up the buffalo robe. "Charity, where are you?"

There was no answer and she turned impatiently to a young woman who had taken a step nearer and was regarding her with curiosity.

"The little one? Where is she? Where is the yellow-haired girl?"

The young woman went on staring at her out of bright inquisitive eyes.

"Very well! I'll find her myself!" Her patience snapping, Deborah elbowed her way through the crowd and set off across the frosted grass.

A moment later there were quick strides behind her and Adam's lean hands fastened on her shoulder, jerking her round to face him, tearing the thin stuff of her grey dress.

"A squaw with spirit is highly prized," he said, "but I'm not going to chase you all over the canyon!"

"Let me go!" She spoke through gritted teeth. "Let me go, you – you ignorant, savage, miserable—"

Her words ended in a gasp as she was seized and flung across his shoulder as easily as if she were a doll. Speechlessly she pummelled his back with her fists, the breath sobbing in her throat as he turned and made his way back to the hut with the crowd following.

This time he kicked the door shut and threw her down on the pile of skins and bright blankets with such force that she lay gasping, too breathless to make a sound.

"You would get a good beating for that if you were a Navajo," he observed tensely.

"I'm not a—" Her feeble protest was smothered by his mouth as he pressed her back.

Struggling against him, she contrived to reach the sheathed knife in the pocket of her skirt and tried to pull it out, but even as her fingers grasped the hilt his own fastened upon her wrist in a steely grip, and the weapon spun across the bare floor.

"Kill me, and you'd not live an hour," he said.

"Please. Oh, please!" Suddenly she found herself crying, the tears sliding down her face. "Not like this! Let me go to the women instead!"

"Did you want me to court you with bouquets of flowers and invitations to the dance? I've been out east and seen much courtship and little honest emotion!"

Wriggling, her cheeks damp with humiliating tears, Deborah ducked her head and sank her teeth into his wrist. He slapped her aside lightly, insultingly, and she heard the tearing sound of her dress as he ripped it from neck to waist. Her round breasts, unencumbered by stays, were exposed to his gaze, and in a final, futile effort at modesty she tried to squirm aside, but his hands pinned her down and his seeking mouth was on her awakening flesh. And she lay, unresisting, as he impatiently discarded his own garments, his eyes never leaving the twin globes of her white breasts.

Something within her that lay deeper than reason was opening like a parched flower to the rain. There was a piercing pain more exquisite than anything she had ever imagined and life thrilled through her veins and nerves, whirling her into a place where the colours ran together in a singing rainbow and she was safe from all hurt.

"I knew you were my woman," Adam said, pushing back her hair, sweeping his hand the length of her body. "The moment I saw you bathing in that pool I knew, in my blood and bones, that we would come together. I felt it strongly, like a wind blowing through my life. You felt it too, for I saw your eyes following me as I rode away. When Manuelito returns we will be married. You won't fight me on that, will you?"

She shook her head, watching him as he moved about the

room, laying out garments over the stool, pouring steaming water from the pot over the fire into a deep bowl. It was the first time in her life that she had ever seen a naked man, and she had not imagined there could be such delight for her in gazing at another human being. His body, lit by the firelight, was burnished copper, gleaming and rippling as he performed his toilet. Broad shoulders shrugged into the towel as he rose, dripping, from the basin, his long back curving into narrow waist and lean, firm hips. There was a lithe animal grace in his movements that brought desire surging up in her as he reached for his scattered clothes.

"Come and wash." He glanced at her with teasing in his dark eyes. "I cannot lose face by having a sluttish squaw!"

The water, hot and scented with herbs, was delicious. Her shyness gone, she stripped and scrubbed herself, plunging her curly head into the basin.

"Now you look like a flame dancing on the surface of a lake and shaking drops of water out of her hair!" he exclaimed.

"You can say pretty things when you've a mind." She allowed herself to be enveloped in a coarse towel and sat meekly as he ran a comb through her hair, untangling each red curl patiently.

"We have our gentle side," he said.

"The Irish side?" Snuggled in the blanket she looked up at him.

"Lord, no! My mother was a black-haired termagant!" he exclaimed, laughing. "Seventeen years old when my father captured her, and as wild as any Mescalero! He was a peaceable man, given to reasonable argument, but there was little of that around when I was a child. Those pots and pans used to fly around!"

"How dreadful!" She gazed at him in sympathy.

"He adored her," Adam said, laughing. "He thought she was the finest thing the Great Spirit had ever created, and she would never allow anyone to utter a word against him. When she died of the fever, it was as if he had lost the other part of himself. I was ten years old then, and soon afterwards he put me up on my pony and took me to the mission at Santa Fe, and told me I must learn the ways of my white people. I lived with white people for five years, learning, remembering, listening. Then I did some scouting for the Army and I went east to look at the great cities there. And then, eight years ago, I came home again."

"Your father?"

"Had been killed in a Pawnee raid five years before. But my relatives remembered me, and I hadn't forgotten the old ways. I have settled now into the Navajo custom."

"But you said, when we first met you on the trail, that you had all been told to move to the reservation."

"That's true. General Carleton, over at Fort Wingate, has instructions to 'resettle' the Navajo," Adam said, a wry twist to his grin. "This canyon stretches for thirty miles west of the Chuska mountains, and it's fertile. The bulk of the tribe is settled here quite comfortably, with a high standard of living. But that doesn't suit the idiots who sit in Washington! Show a politician a fertile valley and he'll drive a wagon train through it!"

"So you'll not leave?"

He shook his head, his face grave. "This is our land," he said simply. "We held it against the Mexicans and we'll hold it against Star Chief Carleton. If we can get through the winter, there's a chance that when spring comes we can present our case to the Supreme Court. Now, put on your clothes, and we'll go eat. There is to be a feast tonight, to celebrate your being found. Juanita, who is Manuelito's wife, gave me the dress for you."

They were not like any clothes that Deborah had ever worn before, but when she was dressed, she had to admit they were both warm and comfortable. The ankle-length skirt of soft leather was fringed and dyed green, over long buckskin trews. A green bodice laced over her breasts and a woven shawl in tints of yellow and white completed the outfit.

"Let me help you with your moccasins," Adam said,

bending to tie on the shoes. "There! Now you look like a princess! We will go and pay our respects to Juanita."

He stood up and held out his hand to her, smiling as if she was already part of him. He had not spoken of love, and she had no way of gauging her own emotions, but she was certain that they belonged together.

The tribe was drawn up in a huge circle in the widest part of the clearing, the older members occupying low stools or piles of blankets, the women grouped together with children dodging in and out between them. Two large fires were being tended in the centre of the clearing and the silence of curiosity had given place to laughter and chatter in a mixture of Spanish, English and the strange, spitting dialect.

From among some young girls Charity, clad in leather skirt and bodice, her fair hair newly braided, darted towards them.

"They've not hurt me," she said in excitement. "I can make some of them understand what I say, but they giggle all the time and hide their eyes. Are you hurt, Debbie?"

"No. No, I'm not hurt."

"You look – different," Charity said. "You look more finished, somehow." Her eyes were puzzled as she sought to analyse the difference.

"Adam!" A plump young woman, with gold bracelets tinkling on her wrists and in her ears, stepped up to them and launched into a long speech accompanied by much smiling and waving of hands.

Adam was listening and then answering her, his voice courteous. As the brief conversation ended he drew Deborah forward, speaking in English.

"Juanita, this is the woman I told you about. This is Deborah Jones."

"Deborah." The young woman pronounced each syllable carefully. "We are happy to welcome you and the little yellow-hair. I am sad that the others were killed, but bad things are often in this world, and good things follow. Now we will eat and dance and be happy again."

She clapped her hands and a babble broke out again as those not already seated scrambled for a place.

They ate with knives and fingers, throwing bones over their shoulders to where a number of small, yellow dogs waited, heaping husks into a pile and collecting them up. The meat was crisply roasted, the peas and beans mashed up into a kind of pudding, the corn sweet. There were apples and pears too, and nuts that Adam cracked in his teeth before handing them to Deborah. She was wedged between him and a thin young woman with a scar on her cheek, who pointed to herself saying, "Blue Fish Woman", and returned to her eating.

Some of the men were chewing lumps of meat, then passing them to the women and children to finish. Adam, catching Deborah's shocked look, took a piece out of his own mouth and offered it to her.

"No thank you!" She looked so offended that he burst out laughing.

"It's a sign of friendship," he said, "and it saves your pretty teeth."

"Thanks, but I can chew my own meat," she said firmly.

"I'm glad your teeth are strong. You'll have no trouble chewing buffalo hides, then," he said.

"Chewing *what*!"

"Buffalo hides. The squaws soften them with their teeth."

"You're joking!"

"Not at all. Mind, the custom's dying out now. But if you don't behave yourself I'll beat you and make you chew hides for a week," he threatened.

"I'd like to see you try." Completely at her ease and full of food, she mocked him back, her eyes sparkling.

The chatter and the laughter were dying, and the younger women were collecting the horn drinking mugs, the thick plates with their wavy patterns of blue and yellow, the piles of shells and corn-husks. Deborah became aware that several pairs of eyes had turned towards her.

"They want to hear your story," Adam said.

"What story?" she asked in bewilderment.

"The story of how you came here, where you come from. It is customary for a newcomer to do this, then the Council decides if they can stay. In your case it's a formal matter, no more, for they know you're my woman."

"But I can't stand up in front of all these people. There are thousands of them!"

"No more than a couple of hundred," he said, grinning. "Get on your feet now and speak up bravely. They all love a good story."

She stood up, clasping her hands together tightly to stop their trembling, and heard her own voice, thin and weak in the frosty air, gaining strength as the circle of listening faces grew more intent.

"I came from England," she said, "in a big ship. I was only a little girl then, but I can remember the water all round and the ship going up and down. My father and mother were with me. But they died of the fever when we'd been in America only a few years.

"Two neighbours, friends of my parents, took me in – John and Sarah Laycock. They were good people. Kind people. John Laycock wanted to go out into the Painted Desert to take the Word to the Indians there, and we set off in a wagon, and travelled for months and months. Then Utes came and burned the wagon and killed the Laycocks. Charity and I were down by the river, and they didn't see us, so we started to walk. We walked, and slept, and walked again, and so came here."

There was a silence as Adam finished his translation. Then a tall Indian, his face seamed with experience, rose to ask haltingly, "What is this word you talk about? What is this word?"

"Word of – the Bible," Deborah said haltingly. "You know, about God and the right way to live, and what's wrong and right."

"We know that now," the Indian said, looking puzzled.

"Well, that's all, then." Deborah spread her hands and sat down, feeling foolish.

There was a murmuring that buzzed through the assembled people. Then Juanita stood up, her earrings glinting, her voice warm and resonant as she spoke in the dialect that Deborah was determined to learn.

"What is she saying?" Deborah whispered.

"She speaks as the wife of Manuelito, saying that in her opinion you ought to be allowed to stay here. She adds that you are young and will probably bear fine sons," Adam whispered back.

Someone at the other side of the circle called a question, and Juanita, turning slightly, translated it. "Will the pony soldiers come to seek you?"

Deborah shook her head, feeling the chill of loneliness as she replied, "Nobody will have missed us at all. The Laycocks had no family except Charity."

Juanita spoke rapidly again, and there were more murmurings, and a general nodding of heads. "The dancing will begin soon," Adam said. "It will be a welcome dance for you and Charity."

"The Laycocks never approved of dancing," she began.

"The Laycocks are dead," he said, his eyes holding hers steadily. "They are gone, Deborah, and you must learn other ways now. It would be a terrible insult if you were to refuse to watch."

"I suppose so." She gave a little shrug as she relinquished one of the Laycocks' most firmly-held principles, and turned her attention to the leaping, whirling young men.

The woman called Blue Fish said something to her nearest neighbours and they laughed, covering their mouths with their hands and staring with bright eyes at Deborah.

"They have given you an Indian name," Adam said, looking pleased. "They say you are Laughing Flame, because your hair is fire-coloured and curls around itself. They never saw hair like it before."

"I never was a beauty!" Deborah began crossly, but his hands covered hers and his voice was gentle as he answered,

"You are my woman, Laughing Flame. That is all that need concern you."

CHAPTER
FOUR

"ARE we going to live here for the rest of our lives?" Charity asked.

The two girls were walking together, shawls wrapped tightly about their heads and the lower parts of their faces, for the wind was bitter and snow had been falling steadily for days.

"Unless the people agree to move to the reservation," Deborah said.

"But we're white. White women don't live on reservations," Charity said.

"I think some missionaries do. Don't you like it here? I thought you were happy." Deborah peered anxiously into her companion's face, for in the two weeks since their arrival Charity had seemed busy and contented.

"I do like it here," the younger girl said quickly, "they're not as I thought they'd be. They're like real human beings, not like the ones who – who burned the wagon and killed my parents. I *do* like it here."

"Then what troubles you?" Deborah asked.

"Debbie, you live in Adam's house," Charity said. "I mean, you live with him as if you were his wife."

"We're to be married tomorrow by Herrero Grande."

"According to Navajo rites—"

"Because there is no minister here. Later on we'll have a Christian ceremony."

"I'm not saying anything about that," Charity said hastily, "I think an Indian wedding will be perfectly lovely, and you and Adam have such a neat house."

"Then what is it?" Deborah persisted.

"The other girls," Charity said, colour rising in her face.

"They talk about their sweethearts, and the babies they're going to have, and – I'm past fourteen, Debbie, and I can't talk about those things."

"You're too young to talk of marrying," Deborah scolded.

"Indian girls grow up faster."

"Some of the young men are rather handsome," Charity said. "Have you noticed – no, you won't have noticed because you never see any man clearly except Adam! But they are good-looking, and I've seen them watching me. They've named me Yellow Bird. I think that's a pretty name, don't you?"

"Very pretty, and you're a pretty girl," Deborah returned affectionately. "But you've lots of time before you need to bother your head about young men. In a year or two you might meet a pleasant young white man who wants to marry you, and then you'll be glad you didn't take the first man who looked twice at you."

"Do you like being married?" Charity asked. "Mother told me once that being married was a strange and wonderful thing."

Deborah's mind flashed back to recent nights when she and Adam had seemed to be the only people who mattered in the whole world as they rose together to new heights of unimagined bliss. "Very strange and very wonderful," she said softly. "It isn't something to be rushed at or seized before its time."

She broke off, her eyes widening in horror. They had reached a group of small boys who stood in a circle, their bared arms outstretched, little flames dancing on their flesh. "For Heaven's sake, what are you trying to *do*!" Frantically she scooped handfuls of snow to quench the flames.

"They are training to be warriors," Adam said, coming forward out of a nearby hut.

"At that age? The little one there is no more than six years old," Deborah said indignantly.

"Navajo boys must learn to endure pain without flinching," Adam told her. "They put sunflower seeds on their arms, light them, and stand without moving until the flame burns down to the skin. It is a game for them now, but one day they will need to be brave men."

"It's barbaric!" Deborah exploded.

"In a savage land such customs are necessary," he said, looking amused. "And it is the custom too for females to occupy themselves usefully. Why are you two strolling about?"

"We were wondering what's going to happen," Deborah said. "There's been talk of going to the reservation, hasn't there?"

"From Delgadito, yes." Adam waved Charity back towards the maidens' quarters and took Deborah's arm as they walked on. "He is responsible for the old people, and he's concerned about their getting through the winter. Our supplies are lower than they should be, and many of our cattle are being picked off by Utes and Mexicans. He feels it might be a wise move to take the old ones to Fort Wingate. They would be sure of rations through the winter, and Delgadito can send back a report of the conditions at the Bosque Redondo."

"You don't agree?" She caught the inflection in his voice.

"I stand with Manuelito and Barboncito in this," Adam said. "As a nation we are nearly ten thousand strong. Stay together and we remain strong – but once let us begin to divide into little groups and we will be swallowed up. I have seen it happen before to other tribes."

"Then we stay here?"

"In the land that was ours long before the first settlers came. This is a fertile valley, Debbie, and we have worked very hard to cultivate it. Do you believe it would be right to give everything up tamely because General Carleton orders it?"

"No, I don't," she said with decision. "I think we have every right to stay here."

"There's my brave squaw!" He took her hands, laughing down at her.

"Not until tomorrow," she said primly. "Tonight I'll sleep in the women's quarters. Juanita tells me it is the custom even if the couple have lived together."

It would be a strange wedding with neither ring nor minister, and the feast that followed would be a meagre one, for supplies had been carefully husbanded to last out the winter. The soldiers had already destroyed much of the harvest and what remained had to be shared. There were other Navajo camps scattered in the mountains and the people there were in worse case, some of them already eating mule.

Yet there was no lack of good cheer on the following day when she came out of the women's quarters and walked between the long lines of assembled Navajos to the mound on which Herrero Grande stood with Adam at his side. Deborah could sense the goodwill emanating from the silent spectators as she and Adam had their wrists nicked and bound together in a red cloth while Herrero Grande, in broken English, pronounced them man and wife. Scarves of black, white, red and yellow were hung about their necks, to symbolise the four corners of the world, and Juanita scattered a little grain over their heads that the marriage might be fruitful.

The solemnities over, the festivities began in earnest. A wedding was an occasion when the young girls might choose their own partners, counting coup on the young man they fancied with the ends of their shawls. Deborah, sitting with Juanita, saw Charity, her round face alight with mischief, flick a slim boy on the head and back off slowly, feet tapping, as he rose and advanced towards her.

"The boy is Nino," Juanita said. "Good boy. Kind to his horse."

"She's only a child," Deborah said.

"Yes, very much a child." Juanita looked sadly at Charity as one might look at a mentally backward person and then patted Deborah comfortingly on the arm. "She will grow into a woman very quick," she said.

"Not too quick, I hope," Deborah muttered, wondering if

Charity realised that she was taking part in a courtship dance.

The youngsters were moving aside and squatting on the piles of skins and blankets laid on the frozen ground. The snow had held off for a while and a faint ray of sunshine struggled through the heavy white clouds.

The drums and reed pipes took on a new rhythm, a strange, haunting beat that made Deborah shiver without knowing why. From the throats of those assembled rose a sweet, high humming. A young girl, her braids tied with red ribbon, ran into the clearing and began to dance, her hands outstretched, her eyes half closed. She was joined by a young man, whose fingertips touched hers as they circled.

"This is the Beauty Chant," Adam whispered. "It is one of the prettiest of our legends. The girl is Glispa, dancing in the meadow with her twin brother. In a moment the Snake Man will come, to lure her away to the land beneath the lake."

A third figure, painted in rings and spirals of black and yellow, had leapt into the clearing as the pace of the drums quickened. The girl had paused on tiptoe, and now, as her partner sank sleeping to the ground, she began to imitate the movements of the Snake Man, her hips undulating, her hair swinging free as she pulled out the ribbons and followed the Snake Man out of the circle beyond the fire.

"You must not be unhappy," Juanita said, "the story has a good ending. She is two years with the Snake people and learns many wise things. Watch now and you will see."

The supposed brother was lamenting, his high wailing echoing from wall to wall, his clenched fists beating his head. Into the circle the girl leaped, her hair entwined now with long strings of tiny beads, a cup in her hands from which she sprinkled water as she stamped and twirled in time to the beating of the drums.

"She brings the art of healing to mankind," Adam said, "and heals first the grief of her brother. Now they dance together, round and round in the sacred circle."

It was beautiful, Deborah thought, her own foot tapping as

she watched the leaping figures and felt the sweet, wild melody become part of herself.

Adam touched her on the arm, his glance mischievous as he whispered, "Now is the time for you to run away and hide!"

"Run away! Why should I do that?" she demanded.

"Because the bride must pretend great reluctance," he explained. "I will give you a start of one hundred and then I will run after you."

The others were beginning to stamp their feet and the women were covering their faces with their shawls and moaning loudly.

Deborah sprang up, pulling her own shawl tightly around her and began to run out of the circle, away from the fire, past the wooden houses and staked, moss-packed peach trees. She ran fast, skimming the frozen ground, heading for a narrow path that twisted up to a ledge overlooking the enclosure where the mules were penned. There were many such paths and ledges cutting into the soaring walls of the canyon, and she had even seen small children clambering about among the high rocks like little monkeys. She began to climb, pulling herself up by the handholds as her feet slipped on the ice, crouching down behind a concealing rock as she waited for the others to find her.

After a few minutes she heard the laughter and chatter as they swarmed beneath her. It was unlikely that she would be able to remain concealed for long, and she felt a little surge of pleasure at the realization that capture, in these circumstances, would be a joyful affair.

"*Hoka hey! Hoka hey!*" One energetic lad was charging the rocks with a band of small companions. She peeped out cautiously and saw the smallest of them look up and point in triumph.

Adam had reached her in an instant, pulling her to her feet, slithering with her to level ground again where they were surrounded by the children, jumping up and down and shrieking with hysterical excitement.

"You didn't pick a very clever hiding place!" Adam grinned.

"I wasn't trying to," she retorted, and smiled up at him, snuggling into the warmth of his arm.

He was looking past her however, narrowing his eyes towards the entrance to the canyon. A Navajo, muffled in fur, was riding fast along the track, and one glance at his face told Deborah that the last thing on the newcomer's mind was a wedding.

He swung himself to the ground and the others pressed about him, questioning him, their own expressions reflecting his.

"What is it? Has something happened?" She tugged at Adam's sleeve but he put her aside and went up to the man, questioning as rapidly as the rest.

"Something is wrong," Juanita said, coming up to Deborah. "Kintpuash is one of our best scouts, and would not come back to camp for small reason."

"Adam, what is it?" Ignoring the faint frowns of the other women she pushed her way to him.

"Kintpuash says that notices are being put up by the pony soldiers all along the trail," Adam told her. "He pulled one down and brought it to show us."

"What do the words say?" The tall man who had danced the part of the Snake spoke in heavily accented English.

"It is written in English and in Spanish." Adam frowned at the torn billboard. "Reward of twenty dollars for every Navajo scalp or Navajo steer taken to Fort Wingate. It's signed by General Carleton."

Juanita was loudly translating the message, and out of the shocked silence that greeted the words rose shouts of anger.

"We must ask for a Council," Adam said curtly, taking Deborah's hand and beginning to hurry back towards the fire.

The children, as if aware that the jollities had ceased, trailed disconsolately behind their elders.

"Council not for womans," Blue Fish said to Deborah, pulling at her other hand.

"Juanita is going!"

"Juanita Manuelito's woman. Very wise head."

"I have a very wise head too." Firmly she detached herself from Blue Fish's clinging fingers and followed Adam into the circle.

There seemed to be a set procedure, as the men seated themselves, pulling blankets around them, and most of the women squatted at a little distance. One man, a broken nose detracting from otherwise regular features, stood up and began a long dissertation to which the others listened with varying degrees of attention.

"He is reminding us of the days when we grazed our cattle and grew maize and hunted the buffalo in peace," Adam told Deborah. "He is reminding us that we take no scalps and kill our enemies cleanly and quickly."

"What has that to do with the matter in hand?"

"Nothing, but it is the custom. Hush now!" He pressed her hand as another rose to speak.

It was as formal as a Church Meeting, Deborah thought with a twinge of amusement, as the speeches continued. Each speaker was heard politely, interrupted only by murmurs of "*Hetchetu ahoh*" and much nodding of heads. Only some of the younger men shuffled their feet impatiently, muttering behind their hands.

Then one, bolder than the rest, rose in his place, calling out something and pointing at Deborah. Adam was on his feet at once, expostulating stormily, his voice ringing into the attentive silence.

"El Sordo believes we may gain some advantage if we let the soldiers know we hold two white women," Juanita said. "It is a bad thing to say. You are here of your own will, and such talk brings dishonour."

Manuelito, long moustaches drooping over his set mouth, was on his feet, adding his own opinion. Deborah sat tensely, wishing desperately that she could understand the language.

Surely she could not be used as a hostage on her wedding day! She tried to catch Adam's eye, but he was speaking again, forcefully, his expression passionate.

"You should go to your house," Juanita said, her voice low and kindly. "They will talk for many hours yet, but you must make ready for your bride-bed."

She would have preferred to stay, but her hands were growing numb with the cold and Adam was still arguing, not even turning his head as she rose and went quietly away. The light was fading fast and the younger children were being scooped up and carried away by their mothers. Somewhere beyond the rocks a coyote howled and was answered by its mate.

Indoors she built up the fire and kindled the tallow lamp that hung on a chain from the rafters. The low bed was neatly made, a couple of extra skins laid on the floor, the shutters closed. On the shelves Adam's possessions were tidily arranged. They were few enough, Deborah thought affectionately, her eyes dwelling briefly on each in turn. His rifle, a box of shells, a curved hunting knife, his bow and quiver of arrows, clean shirt and breeches, leather money pouch, a string of amber touch beads. The few items were indicative of a simplicity of life that not even the Laycocks had matched.

She stripped off her own garments and, wrapping herself in a buffalo robe, sat down near the fire to wait for the coffee to boil. It was quite dark and snowing hard when Adam returned, bringing with him a flurry of snowflakes, blowing his hands as he stamped on the floor. She longed to question him about the Council, but wisely held her tongue, pouring coffee and helping him off with his thick, snow-soaked jacket.

"Good girl!" He spoke warmly, gulping the hot coffee and stretching his long legs to the blaze. "I began to think we would be there till dawn!"

"Has anything been decided?" she ventured, noting the little frown between his dark brows.

"Nothing to my liking," he said moodily. "If I were even a sub-chief instead of a tracker scout I would carry more weight in the Council. As it is I must bow to the decision made."

"What is that? Are Charity and I to be held hostage now?" she asked.

"El Sordo is a young fool," he said. "If someone is going to come up with an idiotic idea it will be El Sordo! Fortunately he can easily be turned aside from his course of action. We hold the laws of hospitality as sacred, and those who come of their own free will have the right to leave or stay."

"So what will happen?" she wanted to know.

"Delgadito will take five hundred of the old and sick into Fort Wingate. Captain Chacon is liaison officer there and he's a sympathetic man. If anyone can persuade Carleton to treat them with humanity it is Chacon. In any event, the Army will have the expense of clothing and feeding them throughout the winter."

"You don't agree?"

"I believe we should look after our own," he said, frowning into the dregs of his coffee. "I went to Fort Laramie once and saw the Cheyenne there who'd given up their old ways and were living on handouts from the garrison. Laramie Loafers, the soldiers called them. The men were sodden with drink and the woman degraded."

"We saw some women like that at Fort Dodge," she remembered.

"Then you'll understand what I mean. Pour me some more coffee. I'm as dry as a bone."

She obeyed silently, accepting the fact that at this moment he was not interested in her as a woman. She was merely the receptive ear into which he poured his brooding thoughts.

"The general opinion is against me," he said, "but Manuelito thinks as I do. Men who take Navajo scalps are not to be trusted."

"Then what is to happen?" she asked.

"The old people will go with Delgadito. The rest of us will

dig in here for the rest of the winter. Some will ride south to seek help from the Chiricahua Apaches."

"Apaches!" She looked at him in alarm.

"Since Mangan was murdered by the soldiers his son-in-law, Cochise, has emerged as a very strong leader," Adam told her. "The Chiricahua are blood kin to the Navajo and will help if they can."

"It will mean war," Deborah shivered.

"The Navajos were not the ones who began it," Adam said grimly. "We have lived in peace, with no more than an occasional cattle raid to mar that peace. We enjoy a fine standard of living, and we've worked hard for what we enjoy. So naturally they want to force us on to barren land where nothing will grow, and there is nothing to hunt. Men like Carleton are like that, and he takes his orders from like-minded fools in Washington."

"Will you go to the Apaches?" she asked nervously.

"Not unless it becomes necessary. We'll dig ourselves in here and wait out the winter."

"Yes." She spoke thoughtfully, her eyes on the crackling flames.

"Deborah." His own voice was grave as he looked at her. "Deborah, when I said that you came freely and could leave freely, I meant exactly that."

"I don't understand," she said, turning her gaze towards him in surprise.

"When Delgadito leaves you and Charity are free to leave with him," he said. "You would be taken back east on the next wagon-train if you wished."

"You sound as if you wanted me to leave," she frowned.

"I want you to do as you choose." His voice and face were cold as if he set a distance between them.

"You didn't give me much choice when you threw me over your shoulder and forced me here!" she said. "Are you telling me now that you're weary of me? You might have let me know before the ceremony – or has it slipped your mind that we were married a few hours ago?"

She was not angry but she forced indignation into her voice. Anything to take the cold, still look off his face!

"I was wrong to force you," he said, rising and pacing the floor. "I was very wrong to treat you thus."

"Humility doesn't sit well on you, my husband," she said bracingly. "I like it better when you yell at me."

"On our bride-night?" Some of the coldness went out of his eyes. "On his bride-night a man must speak words of love."

"Then speak them to me!" She went up to him, the buffalo robe slipping from her shoulders.

In the firelight they were copper and ivory twined together and the howling of the wind was muted.

"Laughing Flame." He spoke softly, looking down into her face. "All the things I want to say to you are contained in those two words."

"Then do not speak." She put her arms round his neck and he stooped, lifting her, carrying her to the bride-bed and laying her upon it as if she were very precious to him. This time he made love to her slowly, tracing the curves of her slender body with his lips and long fingers, stroking her flesh until her need for him mounted in her like a hunger, and she pulled him to her, twining her small hands in his long black hair, moaning deep in her throat until he entered her and the rhythm of their mutual fulfilment began.

Much later as she drifted off into sleep, she remembered hazily that it would soon be Christmas.

The next morning Delgadito and his people moved out. The oldest and the youngest were strapped to the backs of mules, their heads and shoulders swathed in furs and shawls. There were some nursing mothers, their infants tied to them, and three sick children whose coughing sounded painfully harsh in the raw air. Yet the general atmosphere was one of cheerfulness, even gaiety.

"They have Delgadito's promise that if they are not happy, he will bring them home again," Adam said as he stood with Deborah, watching the bustle of departure.

"Will he be able to keep such a promise?"

"Carleton is not interested in old people and babies," Adam told her. "He wants to pen up the young braves who might cause him trouble later on."

"But we won't let that happen." She spoke confidently, allying herself with his cause.

"We won't let that happen." He patted her shoulder reassuringly.

"Manuelito and Barboncito will ride part of the way with them and do some hunting on the way back," Juanita said, coming up to them. "Our stocks are not good, we must be wise and save what we can."

"Herrero Grande will consult with you," Adam said.

"Herrero Grande is troubled," Juanita said. "He begins to feel it would be better to try to please the pony soldiers."

"Herrero Grande knows what was decided in Council," Adam said sharply. "He cannot choose to alter his mind now."

"If you were to go to the pony soldiers and speak with them in their own tongue," she pleaded.

"If the Council wish it then I will go."

"But they might not let you return!" Deborah said in panic.

"I ride where I choose," he returned arrogantly. "You forget I have white blood and a certain education."

"You're sure they'll remember that while they're scalping you?" she asked sweetly.

"I've ridden scout for the Army. I know Captain Chacon well. A decent man. I wish he held the command instead of James Carleton. The only time I talked with him he informed me that I was tolerated for my Irish blood, but that in his opinion the Navajos were wolves who infested the mountains."

"Then you ought to stay here and not go riding out," Deborah argued.

"It will be decided in Council," he said stubbornly, and

went to speak to Delgadito who was supervising the loading of two pack horses.

"You want to make your man into a woman?" Juanita said.

"I want him to stay alive. Is there anything wrong in that?" Deborah flashed.

"A man must stay alive in his own way," the older woman said. "That is for you to learn. Come, we will go to the women's quarters and I will show you how to weave the cloth we use for our blankets. We have many patterns, and each pattern tells its own story. And we will teach you some of the words in our tongue. Little Yellow Bird is learning quick."

Deborah would have preferred to continue the argument with Adam, but Juanita was drawing her away. She made one final attempt, demanding crossly, "Have Navajo wives no minds of their own, then?"

"Very strong minds." The other laid her finger along her nose, her dark eyes twinkling. "But we know it is not clever to tame a horse with blows. We must use an apple and a lump of sugar, and lead him so lightly he believes he is still running free!"

CHAPTER
FIVE

"AND *chahumpi ska* is sugar!" Deborah sat back on her heels and grinned round triumphantly.

"You work very hard to become a Navajo," Marietta said approvingly.

One of the older women, she had Mexican blood and sported a gold cross about her neck, an heirloom from her Catholic grandmother. She touched it now for luck as she said, "Half a moon gone and the old ones have not returned. The pony soldiers treated them kindly, I think."

"We will hear soon. Adam will come back and tell us."

Adam had ridden out three days before to scout the district. Deborah had wanted to beg him to remain in the safety of the canyon, but at the last moment some deep instinct had stifled her tongue.

"You are lonely in your bed?" Blue Fish asked.

"Yes. Yes, I am."

"When Adam come back you tell him make you big baby. No time get lonely then!"

"I'll do that!" She laughed and the other women laughed with her. They had lost much of their shy formality and were more at their ease with her now. Some of them, she knew, envied her a little for, as far as Indian wives were concerned, she was spoiled. Even the happiest squaw was expected to hew wood and chew hides and break the ice on the pond to get at the water beneath, and a lazy or unfaithful wife could expect a good beating. Deborah was certainly not unfaithful, but by Navajo standards she was inclined to be idle.

"You have deep thoughts?" Juanita enquired.

"I was thinking I don't even know the day," Deborah said.

"It is the Moon of Blowing Snow – what you call December," Juanita said. "In two or three sleeps it will be the Moon of the Frosted Tepee."

"Then Christmas is gone." Neither her own parents nor the Laycocks had approved of a riotous festival, but there had always been a plum pudding and small gifts.

"I have heard of this Christmas," Marietta said in an interested tone. "A Black Robe from Santa Fe came through here once and told us about it. He was a holy man, a very good man. He told some good stories, eh, Juanita?"

"He had a cross like yours," Juanita said. "Bigger than yours. We had to stand in a row and he poured water over our heads. You remember that?"

"*In Nomine Patris, et Fili, et Spiritus Sancti,*" Blue Fish said unexpectedly.

"It was strong magic," Marietta said. "We had a good harvest that year."

"The Black Robe said he would come back," Juanita said sadly, "but he never came. I guess the Utes or the Pawnee got him. I was sorry about that."

"Would you like a Christmas?" Marietta asked kindly. "When would you like it?"

"It doesn't matter. The time is past now," Deborah said.

"Next time round then," Blue Fish said, "in the summer."

"If you like." Deborah wondered if it was worth trying to explain the sequence of the Christian year, and decided it was probably useless. They would listen politely, but her words would only scratch the surface of their minds.

"Riders coming!" Charity, who was threading beads, raised her head.

"It might be Adam!" Deborah rose, pulling her shawl over her head, and hurried outside with the others.

It was Adam, riding in slowly with a small white man at his side. The newcomer wore an Army uniform under his buffalo robe and a slouch hat pulled over his eyes. As they dismounted, Herrero Grande hurried out of his house with outstretched hand and pleasure in his face. "Ropethrower Carson! It is a long time since we talked!" he exclaimed in English.

The white man grasped hands briefly, speaking in Navajo, and the three went inside, Adam nodding brusquely in Deborah's direction.

"Is that *Kit* Carson?" Deborah whispered.

Even in Kansas City the name of the white man who had lived with Indians was a legend.

"He's a good man," Juanita said. "A good strong man who tells the truth. I am sorry to see him in soldier clothes."

"Why has he come?" Blue Fish asked, her voice uneasy.

"To bring word from Star Chief Carleton," Juanita said. "We will hear soon. Will you go to your house to wait for your man?"

"I'll get a meal ready for him," Deborah said, and ran as fast as she could over the snowy ground towards her hut.

There were root vegetables already simmering in the pot over the fire and some bread she had baked that morning. Meat was getting scarcer and the grain had been carefully stored. She put on an extra pot for coffee and hurried to tidy her things up, guessing that Adam was not in the mood to be enchanted by signs of feminine disorder.

In a shorter time than she had expected the door opened and his tall figure bent beneath the lintel. She hugged him fervently, savouring the smell of wet leather and snow that came from him, and then blushed furiously as a voice drawled at his elbow, "Reckon you've gotten yoursen a tasty armful there!"

"This is my wife," Adam said, faint warning in his tone.

"Glad to meet you, ma'am. I done seen a redhead with them squaws and I was curious. Yes, *siree*!"

"Deborah is from England, Kit," Adam said.

"All that way, and ended up in a Navajo camp! She must have some tale to tell!"

"But now is not the time for telling it," Adam said. "Take

a seat, Carson. Honey, pour us some coffee. Will you have some stew?"

The small man pulled off his hat and shook his head. "I'll not deprive you," he said. "Anyways, I can't hang around long. Shouldn't be here at all by rights. If Carleton knew he'd have my hide."

"You signed on for him," Adam frowned.

"Hell, no! I signed on to fight Johnny Rebs and I get ordered into New Mexico to chase Mescaleros into the reservations. Now I'm to do the same with the Navajo. Sent in my resignation, as you know—"

"And then signed on again," Adam interrupted.

"Figured as you was gonna lose anyways, better for you to lose to someone who liked Indians," Carson shrugged.

"We won't lose," Deborah said.

"And that shows how much you don't know about it!" Carson exclaimed. "You can't win – not with my New Mexican volunteers swarming through Arizona. You'll not last out the winter."

"We'll manage." Adam drank his coffee.

"Oh, *you've* stocks right enough!" the other agreed. "But in the other camps they're living on pinon nuts and killing rats and mules! Delagito's people now – they had a real fine welcome at the fort. Good food and blankets and them sick papooses given medicine. Saw it with my own eyes!"

"But you've not seen the Bosque Rendondo."

"Not to say *seen* it, no," the other admitted, "but General Carleton tells me it could be made a real fine homeland."

"And you believe him?"

"He ain't got no reason for lying," Carson said. "Mind, I'm not saying it'd be Paradise, but it's as good as you're likely to get. And sure as hell's hot, you'll not be able to keep this. There's a new gold strike out in California, and these passes will need clearing to let the crowds through."

"And you'll help clear them?"

"A man has to live," Carson said. "The Army pays good wages—"

"Twenty dollars for a Navajo scalp. We heard."

"Now that wasn't my idea!" Carson expostulated. "I done told my men if I catch them scalping I'll have 'em flogged raw. My principles is real strong on that. Scalping is a mighty unsocial habit and I'll not have it."

"But you'll fight Indians? You'll round them up and send them east?"

"I told Herrero Grande and I'm telling *you*," the other said patiently, "I don't want to fight nobody. I want to talk treaty with you all, give you every chance to co-operate."

"You ought to get married and settle down somewhere and leave folk alone," Deborah said hotly.

"Ma'am, I am a happily married man," he said, looking injured. "I have me a sweet little Arapaho squaw, and a beautiful Cheyenne one, and a real Catholic Christian wife in Taos. Yes, siree, I am one happily married man!"

"That's one of the most shocking things I ever heard!" Deborah said severely.

"As far as I'm concerned you can have squaws lined up across the entire country as long as you leave us be," Adam said.

"Figured you'd have more sense than the rest of them," Carson said, cramming his hat back on his head. "You can't hold out against the whole damn Army!"

"Only let us get through the winter and we shall see," Adam said.

"Ten to one you don't make it." The visitor rose, holding out his hand. "You do understand that if Carleton orders me to attack then I'm going to come in fighting? I signed up this time to fight Navajos, and if I can't talk you round then I'll fight. I ain't broken my word in my life to any man, red or white!"

"You'll not stay the night?"

"I'll make tracks now. There's more snow on the way. You want me to talk about this red-headed squaw?"

"You're not to say anything," Deborah said quickly.

"Suit yoursen, ma'am. I won't say nothing about you to

anyone. And I sure wish you luck! Next few weeks you'll be needing all you can get."

He touched his fingers to the brim of his hat and went out again, with Adam following. From the doorway Deborah watched him mount up and ride away, with small groups of Navajos gazing after him in silence.

"Will he really bring Mexican soldiers to attack us?" she asked.

"If he can't bring about a surrender," Adam said, turning back to her, "then he'll carry out Carleton's orders. I don't blame him. A man has to earn a living."

"But you wouldn't do such a thing, would you?"

"Scout for the Army? Not now. I'll stand with my father's people." He touched her arm gently. "Go indoors before you catch cold. I must have a word with Juanita. Manuelito and Barboncito have ridden north to check on the Navajo camps there. If rumour is right, some of them are in a bad way."

His smile promised a long, warm night of intimacy ahead, but Deborah's own heart was heavy as she went back to the fire. The winter would be a long, harsh one and she was feeling more and more uneasy about the spring.

The Moon of Frosted Tepees blew in with gales of snow that blocked doorways and hung heavy from the eaves. The river was frozen and the children tied bones to the soles of their moccasins and skated up and down, screaming with laughter. The mules had been corralled and the ponies were put under shelter. "If we can get through the winter," Adam had said. But every day hungry Navajos from the hill camps were coming into the canyon to be fed on the rapidly diminishing supplies of jerky and root vegetables. Nobody, it seemed, was ever turned away.

Deborah, who had begged a chicken from Juanita, had set it to broil and gone to fill the water-bucket one afternoon. She returned to find the door open and four strange Indians sitting round her fire and carefully sharing out the bird. For a moment she stood flabbergasted and then, as one of the uninvited guests handed her a juicy wing, her temper broke.

"Out!" She seized the besom leaning against the wall and raised it threateningly. "Get out of my house this instant! *Out!*"

They went on staring at her with open mouths, blank bewilderment in their eyes. With renewed annoyance she saw that one of them had wrapped himself in a skin from the bed.

"Thieves! *Ladrone!* Out!" Her voice shrilled higher.

"What the devil's all the caterwauling about?" Adam demanded, stepping in with a pile of logs under his arm.

"These – robbers are eating the chicken!" She tugged angrily at a corner of the purloined blanket. "And stripping the bed! They were here when I got back."

"I hope there's a share for me. It smells marvellous." Adam dropped the logs into a corner and squatted near the fire, talking in rapid Navajo to the oldest of the party.

"A share! Adam, it was for you and me. Juanita gave it to me!"

"These people are from Armijo's camp—"

"I don't care if they're from the Archangel Gabriel's camp," she interrupted furiously. "They came in without so much as a by-your-leave, to steal *our* supper!"

"In times of hardship everything is shared equally," Adam said.

"Without waiting to be invited, I suppose? That is just plain stealing and you know it!"

The man in the blanket leaned across to Adam and began to talk rapidly, jerking his head towards Deborah and frowning.

"What is he saying? He speaks too fast." Still holding the besom, she glowered at them.

"He is telling me to explain to my white-face woman that all Navajo are brothers. One cannot steal from one's brother. If the food belonged to a Pueblo, then it would be stealing to eat it." Adam turned back to the others and spoke in Navajo again.

"And what are *you* saying?" she asked suspiciously.

"That you were very badly brought up and don't understand the customs of my people," he said calmly.

"*Your* people! You talk like an Indian!"

"And you talk like a fool," he returned, his lips tightening.

"A fool, to cook something special for you? It's ages since we had chicken, and now you give it away to the first person who comes along. No, you stand by and let them take it, which is worse!"

"What we have we share," he said coldly.

Pressing her own lips together Deborah sat down on the stool, shaking her head when one of them offered her some meat. Part of her was concentrated upon hating him. He had no real civilisation behind him, despite his Irish mother, and with his black top-knot swinging and his lean brown fingers dipping into a hot stew he looked, at that moment, completely Indian. Part of her was beginning to feel ashamed. The Laycocks would have shared whatever they had without grudging it, and her basic honesty mirrored her as small and mean.

They were rising now, shaking hands, moving towards the door without looking at her. In a moment they would have gone and Adam would have been shamed by an ill-mannered wife.

Hastily she stood up, grabbing the precious loaf of sugar and the bag of coffee beans from the shelf.

"*Chahumpi ska? Pazchuta sapa?*" she asked, holding them up and nodding invitingly.

They hesitated for a moment and then sat down again, their faces warily melting into small, tight smiles. Adam gave her an approving pat on the shoulder and some of her anger drained away. Perhaps, after all, it was more important to build up friendship than to save food, at least Adam was pleased with her. She couldn't avoid a wry, self-deprecating grin at her own inconsistency, for she was still irritated at the loss of her supper and at Adam's bland assumption that she would follow Navajo customs without any argument. As the conversation went on she began to wonder uneasily if they intended to stay all night.

The coffee drunk, however, they rose again, bowing their heads in her direction with much more friendliness, and went out. Adam, closing the door behind them, smiled at her.

"If we need help from them it will be given without question," he told her.

"I still don't think it's right to march in and take what you want," she said stubbornly.

"Poor little white squaw!" he said, laughing, "trying so hard to understand the ways of the ignorant savage! Come to bed, there's a good wife!"

"I'm still not pleased," she muttered, sidling closer and shivering a little in the anticipation of a delicious reconciliation. He made no move towards her, but stood, frowning slightly, his head cocked to the side.

"What is it?" She stopped flirting and gave him an anxious, questioning glance.

"Can you hear anything?" he asked.

"Only the wind blowing down the canyon. What do you hear?"

"The wind. One of White Eagle woman's children's crying."

"Little Coyote has a bad tooth."

"One of the mules is braying. There's a fall of snow from Juanita's roof." With his sharper hearing he identified the little, separate sounds.

"What troubles you?" she asked.

"I don't know." He shook his head, frowning. "But I have a prickling at the top of my nose – that's a sure sign that something is wrong. My mother used to get the same feeling sometimes."

"Come to bed," she invited.

"Later. Think I'll ride up to the rim of the canyon and take a look."

"It's snowing again. You'd not see more than a few yards!"

"I'll take the horseshoe path." He was pulling on his fur again.

"I'll come with you," Deborah said.

"There's no need. I'll be back in a couple of hours."

"We'll both be back in a couple of hours," she said firmly, reaching for her own buffalo cloak.

To her relief Adam made no further protest but pulled the hood over her hair and opened the door. A flurry of snow blew into her mouth as he took her hand, crunching through the snow that lay thickly over the ground. From her house opposite Juanita called, cupping her mouth into the wind, "Do you come to visit?"

"We're going up the Horseshoe to look about there," Adam shouted back.

"Something is wrong?"

"I'm not sure. I'm going to find out."

"I'll tell the others to keep watch!" Juanita yelled, and plodded to her neighbour's house.

Adam took Deborah's arm and urged her towards the corral. Within its thatched enclosure the horses milled restlessly, scenting snow – or something else? She looked questioningly at him, but he was calming two of them, blowing gently into their nostrils, cutting them off from the others.

She was hoisted to the back of the smaller one and clung to the rough mane, waiting while he adjusted the rope bridle. She was still very far from expert on the blanketed ponies that even the tiny children rode with skill.

"I'll lead. Follow close and pull your shawl over your mouth," he ordered.

She nodded, crouching low as they rode into the teeth of the gale. The high banks of the curving path afforded some protection from the wind, but the going was slow and slippery. At a bend in the Horseshoe Adam drew rein, shielding his eyes with his hand as he scanned the length of the canyon.

"Adam, what is it?" she asked.

"Movement." He pointed. "From both ends of the valley."

"Navajos coming in for food?"

"Not with the light glinting on their belt buckles and rifles."

"Soldiers?" She felt a thrill of fear.

"Carson's men," he said tersely, "coming in from both ends. It looks as if he got his orders from General Carleton after all."

She was going to question him further, but he raised his head and sent a cry shivering into the wind. It was repeated from below and suddenly there was movement all over the valley as figures ran from huts and tepees, scrambling in every direction.

"The women and children must be taken to higher ground! Stay here!"

Deborah was almost thrown as he loosed the guiding rope and galloped back down the valley. Now she could hear the steady tramping of many feet, the screams of horses as they plunged with their riders in the deep snow, the yells of the men as they struggled into their clothes and reached for their weapons. There were puffs of smoke and sharp, cracking sounds from far down the valley.

Frozen with horror, she backed her pony against the icy cliff. Below flames sprang up, outlining struggling figures and the wind fanned them briskly, long lines of flame running across the snow.

They were climbing up to the rocks, the babies tied hastily to their mothers' backs, older children hunting about them for stones and pieces of wood to hurl down on the heads of the soldiers below.

There was a terrified confusion everywhere and the snow was falling more thickly, blurring friend and foe. Deborah had a glimpse of Adam, laying about him with the butt of his rifle, and then Nino was pulling at her bridle, his young face frantic as he gasped out, "Yellow Bird! You take her. Ride quick!"

He was hoisting a sobbing Charity up behind her. Someone else was thrusting a screaming baby into her arms.

Above, the path wound up to the rim of the canyon and the snow-shrouded plateau beyond. She found herself riding towards the skyline, clutching the baby with one hand, hoping that the unshod pony wouldn't slip on the ice.

They had reached level ground again and she was riding hard, with other riders keeping pace with her. She had no idea what direction she was taking, but there was a shallow ravine ahead where they could find shelter.

As they reached it Charity, her face distorted with fear, slid into the snow, her voice cracking as she begged, "Debbie, oh Debbie! Are they going to kill us all?"

"Of course not!" Dismounting, the older girl jerked her upright and pushed the baby into her arms. "Stay here! I'm going back for more."

She had not known that she could ride so well or so fast. There was not even time to wonder if Adam were alive or dead.

There was fighting from end to end of the canyon now, and the snow was mingled with billowing black smoke from the burning tepees and wooden houses. The grain store was ablaze, and as she drew rein she saw the black branches of the peach trees catch fire and crackle briskly.

Little Coyote, his cheek distended with toothache, was crawling on his hands and knees towards her. She scooped him up and rode back across the trampled snow.

Fire made the scene as bright as day, and even the wind was muted by the shouting and screaming and rapid patter of musket shots.

"Carleton's scorched earth policy," Adam said.

He had appeared as if by magic at her side, his face grimed with powder, a jagged cut at the side of his head dripping blood down his cheek.

"Cannot they be stopped?" she gasped.

"With rocks and stones and pieces of wood? We have scarcely any ammunition left!"

"But to burn everything! It will mean starvation!"

"We've faced that before," he said grimly. "Go and find Juanita, and make her take shelter! She will stay and fight with the men until she is taken, and we cannot afford to lose such a hostage!"

He slapped her pony on the rump and galloped off into the dark confusion of battle again.

Juanita was on a ledge, fierce joy on her face as she flung stones down, her voice hoarse with cursing. "Adam says you must go to shelter. Manuelito will be angry if you are taken," Deborah shouted.

"I go when I'm good and ready," the chief's wife shouted back. "You go help more children! The Mexican dogs will sell them over the border!"

Deborah rode on down into the valley, her ears ringing with the din, her eyes narrowed against snow and smoke. Ahead of her one of the elderly squaws, who had refused proudly to go with Delgadito, stumbled from a blazing tepee towards a soldier. In her hands she held out a bright shawl, offering it as she cried quaveringly, "No kill. *Por favor*, no kill!"

The soldier ran her through, pulled out the sodden lance, and rode on.

"Evening, ma'am. This is a bad business."

She looked in bewilderment at the small man who had ridden up to her. Kit Carson sat his horse slouchingly, his hat pulled low, a smoking musket in his hands.

"How could you?" she asked, and the anguish inside her was too great to be expressed in screams of rage. "How could you do such things?"

"Orders, ma'am. I signed on to obey orders – as I made plain."

"To burn and destroy, to starve us into submission?"

"You can ride with us now back to the fort," he said. "You ain't Navajo."

"I stay with my man," she said proudly.

"Reckoned you'd say that. Adam got himself a real spunky gal. Give him my regards. Tell him you all had fair warning."

"You can just go to hell!" she said through gritted teeth. "I hope you get scalped!"

"Maybe so, ma'am." He put his fingers to the brim of his hat, and rode off again, shouting a command as he went.

She wheeled about and galloped back to the Horseshoe. From the ledge Juanita, mounted now, called down to her, "Go to your man, Laughing Flame! The soldiers are burning everything that will burn!"

"The peach trees—!"

"We'll not forget that!" Juanita leaned to seize the dangling rope as Deborah edged back up the icy path. "Rope-thrower Carson could have left us the peach trees. Go now. Tell Adam I will come soon."

Smoke rising from the valley, new snow falling from the dark sky, and all the sorrows of the world expressed in the keening of the wind. Sobbing with frustration because there was no remedy, Deborah urged her weary horse into the growing blizzard.

CHAPTER
SIX

"Fourteen killed. Two frozen to death on the high pass. Thirty-two captured. Sixty surrendered."

In Adam's flat recital of facts lay a horror and a bitterness too deep to be expressed. Deborah could offer no easy comfort, for this disaster was beyond the experience of any of them. Bad harvests could be mitigated by help from other tribes and death, coming in the fulness of time, was natural, but this was a grief for which there was no panacea. The Canyon de Chelly had been traversed from one end to the other, the orchards and houses and grain stores burned, the ponies and mules driven off.

The soldiers had returned to the fort. Only an occasional patrol could be glimpsed on the far skyline, rounding up stray Navajos.

"As if we were cattle!" Juanita said bitterly, her dark eyes flashing. "They do not think we are people at all."

"They have only to wait and we will die of the cold and the hunger," Herrero Grande said.

Sheltering in the narrow gully, furs and blankets wrapped about them, they discussed the situation, their grave faces pinched by the cold and the increasing hunger that gripped them all.

This was no formal Council but a meeting at which all, including the women, had an equal chance to speak. The four chiefs had ridden in, leaving other groups encamped shiveringly in the passes around. What food and blankets remained had been shared out and some of the young men had ventured on a hunting expedition though it was doubtful if they would bring much back.

Now Herrero Grande rose to speak, stamping his chilled feet on the frozen earth, his breath white on the bitter air. "I am chief over three thousand, too many for me to feed and clothe. It is better for me to take them in now to get food and clothes from the white soldiers. Delgadito and El Sordo sent word that they and their people have been kindly received at the Bosque Redondo."

"I fear soft words from white soldiers," Manuelito said, "and even if they are true, it is better to live free."

"I stand with you," Barboncito said. "Though I come from the same father as Delgadito and El Sordo I follow the same road as my friend."

"And I, Armijo, stand with you both," the other chief declared. "I will not lead my people into a prison!"

"Then you will lead them to a slow dying," Herrero Grande said fiercely.

Deborah, concentrating hard on the words for the men spoke too fast for her limited understanding, felt her sleeve tugged by Nino. His young face was strained as he whispered in his halting English, "Laughing Flame, you come talk with me?"

She nodded, slipping quietly from her place. At a little distance from the others he paused, his sloe-black eyes pleading. "I am sworn brave to Herrero Grande," he began.

"Yes, I know that."

"If I go with him to the Bosque Redondo, I think of Yellow Bird. Will she come with me?"

"She is too young to be married yet," Deborah said crisply.

"Navajo girls are married at twelve."

"Charity is not a Navajo girl. I cannot allow her to wed before she is sixteen, and that is not for another two winters."

"Then speak for me to Adam-Leap-The-Mountain," he begged. "He can ask Herrero Grande to release me into his service. Then I need not go to the Bosque Redondo."

"Nino, how old are you?" Deborah asked.

"Seventeen summers. Old enough to take a squaw."

"Are there no Navajo girls?" she enquired lightly.

"Many, but they do not have eyes like the sky and hair that is like the silk corn when it springs from the earth," he said.

"Charity knows little of your ways," she objected.

"She learns as you learn," he countered. "I will be a kind husband to her."

"Yes, Nino, I'm sure you will." She looked at him affectionately, noting his sensitive hands and the rather full mouth that might have made him appear too girlish had he not had whipcord muscles and an air of dignity that belied his youth.

"I will give her a fine pony to ride," he said, "and blankets and a new fur. I know I do not have these things yet, but I will get them for her. But I must stay here, not go with Herrero Grande."

"What are you two whispering about?" Charity asked, coming up.

"Nino wishes to swear himself into Adam's service and stay here with us until you're of an age to marry," Deborah said.

"I'm of an age now," Charity said with a flash of resentment.

"Your parents wouldn't have thought so, and I stand in their place."

"But in two winters," Nino said, "we can be married? I will bring you a pony and a blanket and a fur."

"In two winters we will all be dead," the girl said restlessly. "In less than that if we stay here."

"We are not going to stay here," Adam interrupted, joining them.

"Has something been decided?" Deborah asked eagerly.

"After a fashion." Adam frowned as if the decision had not been much to his liking. "Herrero Grande will take his people to Fort Canby and the rest of us will spread out in several directions. Armijo and Barboncito will go to the San Juan, and Manuelito to the Little Colorado."

"And where will we go?" she asked.

"A small group of us will turn south-west to establish contact with the Chiricahua." Seeing a puzzled look on Nino's face he translated rapidly for the boy's benefit.

"Nino wants to swear service to you so that he can stay near Charity until she is of an age to wed," Deborah told him.

"Is this true, Nino?" Adam gave the boy a searching glance.

"*Hetchetu aloh*," Nino nodded.

"And Charity agrees to this?"

"I want to be married now," Charity said, "but Deborah treats me like a child."

"Behave like an adult, then, and we may agree to a wedding in the summer," Adam said pleasantly, silencing Deborah with a look.

"And you will speak to Herrero Grande? Ask him to release me from his service?"

"I will do that." Adam smiled at the boy, stretching out his hand to grip the other's wrist. "But there are many things to consider. You have kinfolk."

"They will go with Herrero Grande," the boy said, "but I will set my life between Yellow Bird's hands, and we will make a new dream together. This I have told them already and they have agreed, but it is Herrero Grande who must make final word."

"I will speak to him for you," Adam said.

"May I walk with Yellow Bird for a short while?" The boy looked at Deborah.

"For a very little while," she said. Nino and Charity linked hands and walked off slowly together, their heads bent, their voices whispering.

"It will be a good marriage," Adam said, gazing after them. "Nino is a fine young man."

"If we survive the winter." Deborah tucked her arm through his and looked up into his face. "Tell me truly now."

"Don't I always tell you the truth?" He looked down at her, his dark eyes tender. "We will live, some of us, but the hardship will be great. These are bad times."

"But will we go to the Chiricahuas? Will they help us?" she asked anxiously.

"Dear Laughing Flame! You begin to sound like Navajo born!" he exclaimed.

"I am Navajo wed," she told him, "and where you go I will go."

"The Chiricahuas are not fond of the white races," he said sombrely. "Their Chief, Mangan, was murdered by white soldiers last year, tortured and bayoneted. He was an old man who had gone to seek peace, and they killed him."

"Who is chief now?" she asked.

"Cochise, his son-in-law, leads them, but he feels great bitterness," Adam said. "I am not sure how he will receive a white woman."

"I will travel under your protection as Charity will travel under mine, and Nino will serve you as he wishes to do," she said steadfastly.

"And I must speak to Herrero Grande." Adam loosed her arm from his grasp and went back to where the others were still talking.

Deborah moved away, her feet crunching in the snow, and made her way slowly to the top of a little rise. From its top she could look out over the surrounding snow locked plateau, its rock seamed by deep cracks in which a few clumps of sagebrush struggled bravely through glinting ice. The distant peaks were frosted with white, the nearer trails deep-rutted. Along these tracks small figures moved slowly, some in groups, with here and there a single traveller trudging over the frozen wasteland.

"They do not wait for the word of their Chiefs," Juanita said, joining her. "Hunger drives them to the forts. Soon many hundreds of our people will be on their way to the Bosque Redondo."

"But when the winter is over they will come back," Deborah said.

"Dear Laughing Flame, you are such a great comfort to

me," the older woman said. "You will go to the Chiricahuas with Adam?"

"Charity and I will both go."

"Then I will send Blackbird with you," Juanita said. "She had an Apache father who could deny her nothing. If you are with her they will look at you more kindly."

"You're very good to me," Deborah said simply.

"I am very fond of Adam," Juanita said. "I remember his mother. I was just a little girl and she was one of the first white women I'd ever seen. I was afraid of her at first. She was very pale, with black hair that curled around as yours does, and a voice that was louder than your voice is. She raised it often, but she had a good heart too, but life has not been easy to him."

"Because he's of mixed blood?"

"He moves between two worlds," the other said. "One day those worlds will meet and mingle, but it won't happen yet. Perhaps you and Adam will help to bring it about."

She touched the girl's arm gently and turned away, pulling her shawl over her head, straightening her shoulders in a little, gallant gesture that went to Deborah's heart.

The next day they broke ranks and separated, Herrero Grande taking his people along the Fort Canby trail, the others going north. Only a dozen of them turned south-west, Adam riding out with Nino at his back. Blackbird, a copper-skinned beauty with hair she could sit on and eyes like pools of black ice, rode with them, sitting her horse as if she were part of it. Her husband had ridden with Manuelito and she was to rejoin him in the spring. At the moment of parting it was of the spring that they all talked, of the time when they would be reunited and build their houses again.

"In the Moon Of Red Cherries we will meet on the Staked Plains," Juanita said, embracing Deborah. "It will be summer then and the bad times melted like the snows. You will see!"

It was hard to picture the snow melted as they rode

through the white wasteland. The wind stung cheeks and lips and froze fingertips, and the frequent squalls of snow blinded them. At night they huddled together in whatever crevice they could find, sharing the food they had brought with them, eating in slow, small bites to make the frugal portions go further.

The great plateau was broken by the rearing mesas, the cliffs carved into fantastic shapes by the eroding wind. It was like the surface of some undiscovered planet, Deborah thought, and shivered, seeing them in her mind's eye as tiny explorers moving beneath an indifferent heaven towards an unknown world.

On the second morning Charity woke, red-cheeked and bright-eyed, calling for her mother. Deborah, shaking snow from her own buffalo robe, heard with anxiety the other's harsh breathing.

"A feverish cold," Adam said briefly, bending to feel Charity's pulse and hot head. "She ought to be under cover with a good dose of coltsfoot and honey laced with whisky inside her."

"Where are we to find such things here?" Deborah asked, fear sharpening her voice.

"There's a trading post a couple of hours away. We can leave her there for a few days." He was hoisting Charity to her pony, where she sat slumped and tearful, her eyes and nose running.

"I will stay with her then," Deborah began, but he shook his head.

"You'll be needed at my side. She'll be safe and warm at the post and Nino can pick her up in a few days' time. Now don't stand arguing while we freeze to death. Mount up!"

She did so, noting that Nino was riding close to Charity, his arm steadying her lest she fall.

"Yellow Bird plenty sick," Blackbird said, glancing at her.

"She has a bad cold and a touch of fever. Nothing more." Deborah spoke irritably, for the Indian girl was spelling out her own unspoken terror.

They were descending into a valley where the snow was thinner, lying in patches on the stony ground. Ahead of them smoke belched from a tin chimney set on the sloping roof of a sturdily erected wooden building.

"Nino, come with me and bring Yellow Bird." Adam dismounted, raising his voice in a shout. "Joe! Hey, Joe!"

From the door of the wooden building a thickset man, rifle raised and aimed, came out, frowning across the distance between.

"Adam-Leap-The-Mountain?" His voice rumbled as he slowly lowered the weapon. "What brings you so far south?"

"Seeking the Chiricahua." Adam walked forward, Nino following with Charity in his arms.

"Hunting party are camped an hour's ride west of here." The man peered at Charity. "How come you've gotten a white wench?"

"She's travelling with us and she's sick. Exhaustion and cold."

"This ain't no hospital," the trader began.

"But you can let her rest up here for a couple of days?"

"Until tomorrow. I'm lighting out myself then. Going to collect more supplies."

"A good night's rest is all she needs. Can you trade us anything now?"

"Cleaned out." Joe spread his hands. "That's why I'm going to pick up supplies. This weather's a bitch."

"But you'll lodge the girl?"

The trader hesitated, then nodded. Nino went past him into the wooden hut, carrying his burden carefully.

"How come you got two white women with you?" Joe demanded, his eyes darting to Deborah.

"She's my wife," Adam said shortly.

"You mean you got yourself a permanent partner!" The other put his hands on his hips, laughing. "Sweet Jehosophat! The worst winter the devil ever sent, the treaty broken, and you decide on a wedding! She must love you a bundle! Ain't that so, ma'am?"

"You don't expect a good Navajo wife to admit it in public, do you?" Deborah retorted.

"Hey, she's a spunky one!" he exclaimed. "You ride on now and I'll take care of the little gal. Is she spoken for too?"

"To me." Nino had come out of the hut and was pointing to himself. "She is for me in two summers' time. Tomorrow I will ride back for her."

"Perhaps I really ought to stay too," Deborah began, but the trader shook his massive head.

"Don't need fussing females," he said. "I can dose her and get the fever down without any help. Just make sure that young buck comes back for her tomorrow."

"I will come." Nino took one long look at the open door and sprang to his pony.

As they rode away Adam leaned to reassure Deborah. "Joe's a good man, and an honest one. He'll take good care of her."

"Isn't it dangerous for him to live out here all alone?" she asked.

"For most men it would be, but Joe never fears anyone or anything," Adam said. "He and Mangan were blood-brothers, and so he is respected by the Apache on that account."

"As they respect you?"

"They tolerate me," he said, grinning, "because of my father's Mescalero cousins. Ride at my side now and hold your head up. The Chiricahua admires courage more than any other virtue."

She nodded, swallowing hard as they rode lower down the valley. They were leaving the deep snow behind them now though patches of it still clung to the high rocks and the wind was bitter. Above its whistling and the thudding of their ponies' hoofs she heard something else, a sound that turned her blood to ice-water, for she had heard it before. The steady pounding of drums broke upon her ears like a death knell.

"They know we are coming," Adam said, and turning, said something in Navajo to Blackbird who immediately kicked her mount into a gallop and sped ahead of them into a narrow ravine that lay in their path.

The others reined in their ponies and waited, pulling their cloaks more securely around them, their expressions grave but not fearful. Deborah tried to imitate them, setting her mouth firmly, staring ahead of her through narrowed eyes. Scraps of talk she had heard when she lived in Kansas City came back to her as she waited.

"The Apaches are the most savage and cruel of all the tribes. The Spaniards taught them the arts of torture and mutilation."

"They say if the Apaches capture a white woman they rape her until she bleeds to death."

Blackbird was returning, flanked by two men clad in buckskins with scarves swathed about their heads. Their long hair was greased and braided, their faces painted with strips of yellow and white.

Adam rode forward slowly, raising his right hand and circling it to the right in the ritual sign of greeting. The others reflected the gesture and the taller of the men stepped forward and began to speak rapidly.

Adam replied in what sounded like Spanish, and then gestured to the others to follow as Blackbird and her companions turned back into the ravine.

Riding slowly between the high crags, Deborah was aware of eyes watching from the nooks and crannies. She kept her own straight ahead and, despite the cold, felt sweat trickling down the back of her neck.

They reached a sheltered space with huts, made of a mixture of clay and small stones, built in a rough circle around a blazing fire. There were more Apaches here, the women rising from their places around the fire to stare at the newcomers. Deborah sensed a muttering among them, and one woman who was carrying a child hastily covered its face with the corner of the shawl.

A slim young man, with a single red feather stuck into his headband, came forward, making the sign of greeting. Adam dismounted and the long, earnest conversation began again. Dismounting with the others, Deborah could not restrain a nervous glance around her. These people were smaller than the Navajo, their eyes slitted, their noses and lips thin. With a shudder Deborah noticed long strands of hair fixed on poles and fastened to their belts. It was the first time she had ever seen human scalps, and her flesh crawled with disgust.

"Deborah, this is Cochise's elder son, Taza," Adam said, turning to draw her forward. "He says he grieves for the tears of his Navajo cousins, but there is little he can do to help. His father is away in the high passes, and others of the Chiricahua are hunting along the Mexican border. But he bids us stay here for as long as we please, to share their food and ceremonies."

Taza had stepped up to her, his hand reaching to pull at her hair. He said something to Adam and the latter smiled, nodding his dark head.

"He says you must not be offended if the people stare. Many of them have never seen fire hair before and they are afraid of her."

"The feeling is mutual," Deborah said wryly.

"They'll not harm you. I explained that you were my wife."

"And Charity?"

"Will be collected in the morning. Come, we'll see to the ponies and then eat."

The thought of food was tempting, but she kept close behind Adam as they went across the clearing towards one of the huts of clay and stone. "This is a guest hogan. We will sleep in this," he told her, stepping within the dim interior.

"All together?" There was dismay in her voice. "When are we going to be alone again?"

"You miss the privacy of our own adobe, don't you?" He turned, holding out his arms and she went into them, lifting her face for his kiss.

"I loved it," she said, her green eyes wistful. "It was like a real home, the first one of my own I ever had. My parents lived in lodgings after we came to America and the Laycocks moved about wherever the Lord inspired them. But the adobe in Canyon de Chelly was my real home. *Our* real home, Adam! And the soldiers destroyed it, made us wanderers and outcasts."

"Not for ever. We'll go back to the Canyon de Chelly one day," he promised. "It may take many months, but we will return."

His words were an affirmation of faith, and she clung to them as she clung to him, taking comfort in their strength.

It was a welcome relief to sleep under cover, with her hunger pangs dulled by roast rabbit and root vegetables boiled and mashed to a pulp. There were flat cakes of maize and a thin sharp-tasting drink that smelled of blackberries.

The Apaches, Deborah noticed, kept at a little distance from her, their slit eyes on her bright hair. They seemed to regard her with as much suspicion as she regarded them, and she had the uneasy conviction that if she had not been with Adam her scalp would soon have adorned Taza's broad belt.

There was in the end some measure of privacy for the others erected a kind of barrier behind which she and Adam could lie, but she was too bone-weary to receive his caresses and fell asleep in the middle of saying goodnight.

It was almost noon when she woke and for a moment she lay, gazing up at the roof of thatched branches, trying to remember where she was. The space beside her was empty and there was the sound of excited voices outside.

Emerging into the first sunshine she had seen for days, her eyes fell on Nino. His pony was lathered with sweat and Nino's face was twisted with rage and grief. Adam's hand was on his shoulder and he was shaking him gently, his own face clouded.

"What is it? What's happened?" Deborah ran up to them, forgetting her nervousness of the little, fierce eyed warriors who clustered round.

"Yellow Bird is gone," Nino said, turning anguished eyes owards her.

"Gone! What do you mean – gone?" she demanded.

"Nino rode over to the trading post to see if Charity was better," Adam said. "Joe told him the pony soldiers came by after we left and took her with them in a wagon."

"To see the pony doctor medicine man," Nino said. "They take Yellow Bird with them to Fort Wingate."

"By force? Did they take her by force?"

"No, no." The boy shook his head. "She left word with Joe that she would be at Fort Wingate and wait for me there. So now I must ride there."

"So now you must do nothing of the sort!" Adam interrupted firmly. "If you go to Fort Wingate they'll send you to the Bosque Redondo with the others."

"I will tell them that Yellow Bird is my woman promised, and they will let me come back with her."

"They are more likely to put you in gaol, and send Charity back east," Adam said.

"But she is my woman promised!"

"And knows it! That is why she left word for you that she will wait at Fort Wingate," Deborah put in swiftly. "One day, before many months have passed, we will be able to go to the Fort and claim her. You will make her your wife then."

"You must earn your bride by waiting and working as she will do," Adam said.

Nino looked from one to the other, his eyes brightening a little. "Do you speak truly?" he asked slowly. "I am not a child."

"No, you are my man sworn," Adam said. "To such men I do not tell pretty tales of comfort. I tell true words to bring out the strength that is in them. You will claim Yellow Bird again when the time is ripe."

"It will be a long waiting," said Nino, "but at the end of the time I will make Yellow Bird my woman true. I will take her bride-gifts and she will come out of the fort to meet me.

Joe said she wept much when she went with the pony soldiers."

"Her tears will become joy when you meet again," Deborah assured him.

The Apaches were questioning Adam and he was answering in a mixture of Spanish and sign language. "They want to know if Nino's woman is to be brought back at once by force," Adam explained. "A raiding party would enliven the cold season for them, but it's wiser to wait. Nino can prove himself a man in the months ahead, and it's better for Charity to be in a safe place. I begin to feel that you too would be safer—"

"With you!" she interrupted. "My place is with you."

"Then we ride with the Chiricahua until the good season comes again," he said, and she smiled, lifting her chin, trying not to notice the dangling scalps.

In the days that followed she tried also not to notice that Adam paid less attention to her than he had ever done. His days were spent with the other warriors and at night, in the limited privacy of their sleeping space, he frequently turned away and slept after only the briefest goodnight.

"He has much on his mind," Blackbird said, watching the expression on Deborah's face as Adam rode out of camp one day.

"One of the things on his mind ought to be me," Deborah muttered.

Deep down, she was aware that she was being unreasonable. All wives could expect to be taken for granted after a while, but she had been quite certain that Adam would be different. Now it seemed that he took more pleasure in the company of Taza and the other Apache leaders than in her own embraces. This morning he was riding out, waving casually as he passed, without even bothering to tell her where he was going.

In a decidedly disgruntled mood she picked up the wooden bucket and made her way towards the creek. One of the Apaches was already there, laid full length with hand cupped to catch the rippling water. As she approached he raised his head, hesitated, then dipped his hand beneath the surface again and nodded in invitation.

For a moment she hung back, repelled by the thick paint daubed across the brave's face and the greasy hair that hung down to his shoulders. But she had offended custom before by being rude to uninvited guests, and now that she was with the Chiricahua she would lose nothing by being polite. Setting down the bucket, she knelt on the bank by him, bending her head to take the water from his palm. The next instant his arms had reached out and seized her, and she was being tumbled to the grass, her cries stifled by a grimy hand.

There was the pounding of hooves, a voice raised hoarsely, the glint of sunlight along the blade of a knife, and something caught her a glancing blow across the temple that spun her into dizziness. Struggling to her feet, shaking her head to clear it, she saw Adam, kneeling athwart the recumbent Apache, knife at the other's throat.

"Adam! Oh, Adam!" Sobbing with relief, she started towards him, but his voice checked her.

Without taking his eyes from the other he said sharply, "Get back into the adobe!"

Gathering together her skirts, Deborah fled back across the encampment into the guest hogan and crouched tremblingly on the pile of skins that served as a bed.

It seemed an age, but was probably no more than a few minutes before Adam's shadow darkened the entrance, and she sprang up, letting the shocked tears pour down her face, waiting for him to take her in his arms. He made no move towards her, however, but stood, blazing-eyed, his voice snapping out words like bullets.

"Are you completely out of your mind, or is it your intention to humiliate me?"

"He tried to rape me," she sobbed, but his voice cut through her angrily.

"He did what any man will do if he receives encouragement!"

"Encouragement!" Her own voice rose. "I was not—"

"Kneeling by him! Drinking water from his hand! Are you so bone stupid you cannot see that that was encouragement?"

"You should have killed him for insulting me," she flashed.

"I kill no man for trying to take what has been offered," Adam interrupted. "You are not among whites now, but among people with a high code of honour, and you will live according to the rules or suffer the consequences."

"Don't you threaten me!" The tears drying on Deborah's cheeks, her eyes narrowed ominously. "I'm no squaw to be taken when you're in the mood and beaten into submission when I displease you!"

"And I am no tame husband to be led by the nose at your whim!"

"My whim! When did you ever consider my *whim*?" she enquired, as angry as he was. "These past weeks you've scarcely noticed me. You bring me to live among savages, and then you ignore me and spend all your time with them, riding out to the hunt, smoking the peace pipe—"

"Would you prefer me to sit and spin with the women?"

"I thought I'd married a man capable of civilised behaviour!"

"And I thought I'd married a woman of good sense, not a silly child who demands constant amusement."

"Perhaps my standards are higher than those of a squaw!" she cried angrily.

"Whatever level they're on, your standards are certainly not mine!" he retorted.

"So!" Deborah drew a deep, quivering breath, her fists clenched at her sides. "So I am to be completely subject to you, am I? I am to be good, and obedient, and hold myself in readiness for those odd moments when you decide to slake your desires on me."

"You were always willing!"

"Well, not any longer!" she said furiously. "In future

you'll not come to me whenever you've nothing better to do. I'll not be picked up and put down like a – a soup kettle."

"In future I'll not trouble you at all," Adam said, his face hard and unyielding. "Stay in here for the rest of the day while I soothe the feelings of your would-be suitor! And from now on, keep your inviting ways to yourself!"

"I'll not be inviting you," she said chokingly.

Adam raised a sardonic eyebrow, his lip curling as he replied, "If I choose to take you, my dear wife, I'll not wait for an invitation, but quite frankly, you're not proving worth the effort."

He had gone before she could reply, and for a moment every impulse urged her to follow him and make up the quarrel. Then her own mouth set in an obstinate line. Let him stand by his word if he could. For her own part she would teach him a lesson and make no attempt to heal the quarrel. And having decided that, she was tempted to start crying all over again.

CHAPTER
SEVEN

AFTER six months among the Chiricahuas Deborah had grown accustomed to their fierce looks. The paint they wore, their grease-smeared braids, even the scalps at their belts were merely part of their general appearance, distinguishing them from the taller Navajos with their red-bound top-knots. Even their ways seemed no longer strange, for a harsh environment bred toughness in a nation and their cruelties had in them something of the flavour of a childhood in which pain has no real meaning. There had been no more quarrels between herself and Adam, but he had not tried to make love to her since the day she had drunk from the Apache's hand. On the surface they lived in amity, but it was a façade without tenderness or shared understanding, and at night she rolled herself into a cocoon of blanket and lay, tense and wakeful, waiting to repel a touch that never came.

They had moved from camp to camp, sleeping in the hogans of clay and stone, then riding on and leaving the villages cleared of rubbish for those who would come after. To leave a place fouled or littered was a serious matter.

"For dirt brings sickness," Blackbird said. "White people cannot understand that fact." Blackbird, being only part Chiricahua, talked often to Deborah, unlike the other Apache women who kept their distance, covering their mouths if she came too close. "They think, if you breathe on them, they will have children with fire hair," Blackbird said, giggling. "They have very strange ideas, these squaws."

Deborah laughed with her and then they were abruptly grave again, the white girl regretting the fear that put barriers between people, Blackbird thinking of her husband whom she had not seen for many months.

News filtered to them slowly, carried by scouts and the occasional trapper. Once Cochise himself had ridden in with his younger son, Naiche, at his side, and told them of new pony soldiers speaking a strange tongue south of the border.

"French legionnaires brought in to keep Maximilian upon the Mexican throne," Adam said. "They seize their opportunity while the war between the North and South drags on."

Of more interest were the rumours that filtered through concerning the Navajo. "Of the six thousand who went into the forts, five hundred died of cold and exhaustion on the march to the Bosque Redondo," Adam said grimly. "The Army provided twenty-three wagons for them and then commandeered them for other use. Manuelito and Armijo went to talk to Captain Carey, and he persuaded Armijo to take his people in, but Manuelito went back into hiding along the Little Colorado."

"Now that summer is here it will be easier to hold out," Deborah said.

"You always look on the bright side, don't you?" He gave her a somewhat absent-minded smile, and she knew he was still thinking of his father's people herded along the freezing trails to a doubtful destination.

They were to rejoin Manuelito in the Moon of Red Cherries.

"There is to be a big Sun Dance," Nino told her. "We do not have our own, but we are invited by the Sioux and the Cheyenne. It will be a time of great magic."

"There is no such thing as magic," Deborah began, and then paused, shrugging ruefully at the disbelieving look on the boy's face.

All the Indians believed in the powers of magic. The world itself had been peopled by magic when First Woman scattered grain over the earth and each seed sprang up into a human being. The rain came down through the magic of the rain spirits and the wind blew through the magic of the thunder spirits. Every tribe had its own totems and taboos. There was good magic, which belonged to the Red man, and bad magic which the white man had carried with him from the east. And sometimes a thing could be both good and bad. The east was the way the white man had come, but it was also the gateway to knowledge, and the moon was Lady of Birth and Death.

With some vague idea of honouring the memory of the Laycocks, she had tried as soon as her command of the language was sufficient, to tell them something of Christian beliefs. No missionary could have had a more attentive audience as they squatted about her, rapture on their faces, but nothing seemed to make the impression she had hoped. Taza pronounced Judas "one clever-brained fellow," and Chato kept asking how many scalps the disciples had taken. At the end they had stamped their feet and clapped their hands, assuring her she told good tales.

"Not true, but good. Very funny," Taza said kindly. "That squaw dancing and getting John Baptist's head – my! that made me laugh!"

Instead she asked Nino now if he had had any word of Charity. "Kintpuash got through the patrols," he said eagerly. "Yellow Bird is still at the fort. He could not get near enough to speak, but she waits there and is well again."

"And you are growing fast into a man." She smiled at him, seeing how his features were losing their childish contours, his voice deepening. He had asked her to teach him how to read and she spent part of each day showing him how to cut the letters of the alphabet into the clay, and move them about to make simple words.

"I will make very strong magic with these signs," Nino said, happily scratching with the tip of a stick. "I will learn to make Yellow Bird's name and she will think me very clever."

"She will think you very clever indeed," Deborah assured him.

The Sun Dance was to be a splendid occasion. "In a way it's a Dance of Defiance," Adam told her. "Tribes who normally avoid one another, or even raid, will meet and mingle."

"Not Utes?" She gave him an uneasy look. "I'm sorry, but I cannot meet in friendship with the Utes."

"No Utes, Crows, Paiutes or Rees," he promised. "The Sioux and Cheyenne will be there and there's talk of the Arapaho joining the festivities."

"Festivities!" Deborah exploded. "With war and revolution all round us, with Indians being hunted down and driven into the reservations, how can anybody think of having *festivities*?"

"In times of happiness such events are not always needed, but when times are hard and each day blacker than the day before then the Sun Dance draws people together and gives them new hope," he told her. "You will understand how it is when we reach the Staked Plains."

They travelled in small groups, avoiding the main trails where the soldiers still patrolled. The snow had gone and the bitter wind had died, the landscape shimmered under the hot sun in mile after mile of reddish stone above the grasslands that sprang in brilliant colour, starred by tiny flowers that raised their heads as gaily as if winter had never been.

"This is a beautiful land," Adam said softly, watching her face with pleasure.

"Men ought not to fight over it," Deborah said with passion. "Surely there is room for everybody?"

"The greed for land surpasses the greed for love or knowledge," Adam said gravely.

She rode on with him, the others following, along the winding trails that led down from the high passes to the lush pastures that lay like bright jewels in the stony wastes of the desert. Soon the tepees and wicker huts of those already arrived for the Sun Dance came into view. There seemed to be thousands encamped around the central clearing, and instinctively she pressed closer to Adam as they dismounted and moved into the midst of the throng.

The Navajos with their red-bound top-knots were in

marked contrast to the half-naked Sioux with their headresses of eagles' feathers and the Cheyenne in their loin-cloths, bodies painted and oiled, heads shaven up to the long, braided scalplocks. Deborah fancied that several braves eyed her own red curls wistfully.

There were trees around the valley, their branches green with summer, and a river ran by, its shallows already disturbed by children jumping up and down and splashing one another with the water. Their naked brown bodies and rippling laughter made of the place a kind of Eden. At one side joints of meat were turning on long spits over several glowing fires, and at a little distance from all the activity a long hut had been built out of logs of wood over which branches had been piled. From its low entrance white smoke billowed.

"The sweat hut," Adam said, following her gaze. "The men who are to dance the Sun Dance will go there tonight to purify themselves."

"Will you dance the Sun Dance?" she asked.

"Once is enough," he said, grinning. "Come and meet an old friend of mine. George Bent is the son of William Bent and a Cheyenne woman called Yellow Woman. He and his younger brother, Charlie, are here now. George is courting Black Kettle's niece, Magpie."

The sturdy, light-skinned young man in an incongruous outfit of check shirt, buckskin trousers and a number of feathers stuck into the band of a wide hat, shook hands, his small eyes twinkling.

"Glad to know you've tamed Adam at last," he said pleasantly. "You're a real fine-looking woman, Miss Deborah."

"Thank you kindly, Mr. Bent," she began, but he shook his head.

"George, please."

"George, then." She nodded, smiling. "Is your betrothed here?"

"Right over there." He raised his voice calling, "Magpie!"

A small plump-faced girl, her braids tied with red ribbons,

came over slowly and stood, eyes lowered, a little smile playing about her lips.

"Magpie speaks English well," George said, clapping her on the shoulder.

"Not too good, but I learn quick, study hard," Magpie said in a breathless little voice. "You wish to change your dress? Put new one on?"

"I'd love to change," Deborah said, looking down at her stained and torn dress, "but I don't have any other clothes."

"Fleet Foot, daughter of Spotted Tail, has many dresses and is same size as you. Come! We go to her." Magpie, her shyness fading a little, took Deborah's hand and drew her away from the men to where a number of women were plaiting meadow-sweet into garlands.

One of them, a very pretty girl with heavy blue-black hair coiled about her ears, greeted her with a smile so dazzling that one might have supposed Deborah to be a long-lost cousin instead of a foreign stranger. Magpie was talking rapidly in Sioux, a language of which Deborah found she could distinguish several words because of their resemblance to the Navajo equivalent. She was framing her reply when Fleet Foot turned, speaking to her in English.

"You most welcome to take dress as gift. My father, he gave me many dresses. You take and keep. Come, we see."

She led the way to a large tepee, its interior piled with rugs and blankets. A brass-bound chest held garments which Fleet Foot took out and held up against Deborah. "This will please you much," she said. "Will please your man too."

"It's lovely," Deborah said, stroking the white buckskin dress and leggings with their pattern of black and silver stars and half-moons.

"Moccasins too, and cloak of fur for cold nights," Fleet Foot smiled.

"But these are your clothes. I cannot possibly—"

"You must take. Soon I will have no need of them," the girl insisted.

"No need?" Deborah looked at her in puzzlement, but Magpie was tugging at her.

"Maidens' washing pool there, where reed grass hides from eyes of men. Come!" she invited.

There were several young women washing themselves in the privacy of the deep pool. They stared with undisguised curiosity as Deborah stripped. Her white skin, freckled from long exposure to the elements, and mass of flaming hair, evidently struck them as irresistibly funny, for a few of them giggled behind their hands, and one, bolder than the rest, ventured to stroke Deborah's hair and then rubbed her palms together to see if the colour would come off.

Rubbed dry with a blanket that Magpie produced, Deborah put on the clothes that Fleet Foot had given her, and sat down to pull on the moccasins.

"Pretty. My but you're pretty!" a voice said in English.

She looked up, startled, into a face tattooed in yellow and red after the fashion of many Cheyenne women. The one who had spoken wore the wraparound skirt and bodice of the squaw, but her hair was a faded yellow, her eyes blue.

"You're white!" Deborah rose, holding out a startled hand.

"I was once. My name was Martha then, and I was on my way out west with my folks. Ten years back. Now I'm Green Grass, Little Bear's woman."

"I am Deb— Laughing Flame, woman to Adam-Leap-The-Mountain," Deborah said.

"Is he good to you?" the woman asked.

"I couldn't wish for a better husband," the girl said, her eyes glowing.

"You're lucky. My man beats me," Martha said, hitching her shawl around her shoulders and wandering away.

"Little Bear very bad Indian," Magpie said, looking after her with pity. "Come, we find men again."

Adam was deep in conversation with George Bent and a tall, broad-shouldered Sioux whose gold ear hoops and scarlet cloak proclaimed him a man of importance. Adam broke off as the two girls came up, his eyes admiring as he said, "Now you look like a bride again!"

"A girl called Fleet Foot gave them to me. Such a kind girl!"

"Fleet Foot is my daughter," the tall Indian said in perfect English, looking pleased. "She is indeed the light of my morning, and she will live to be the light of my sunset. Of this I am sure, though the medicine chiefs tell me she has the coughing sickness. I tell them no! She will be strong in a year or two."

Now Fleet Foot's remark about not needing the dress was becoming sadly comprehensible.

"Spotted Tail has great friendship for the whites," Adam said. "He speaks for the Brulé Sioux."

"Not for all. Many of my young men wish to untie their horses' tails and ride the warpath," Spotted Tail said. "Me, I believe it is wrong to try to stop the tide of change. We should learn new skills from the white man, share our women, trade and dance when the sun comes. I spent much time at Fort Laramie before the wars began again. The captain there was a good friend of mine. His children played with Fleet Foot, and the soldiers gave her a little white pony."

"This Sun Dance will do her much good," Deborah said, and Spotted Tail seized her hands, shaking them both enthusiastically as he exclaimed,

"You speak good sense, better sense than all the medicine men put together!"

"Spotted Tail adores his daughter," Adam said, as they walked to the space reserved for the Navajos. "She is delicate and everybody knows she will not live to be married, but he will not have it so."

"There is a white woman here," she remembered. "Her Cheyenne husband beats her, she says."

"Not all Indians are saintly, you know," he reminded her.

"I think of the Utes who burned the wagon and killed the

Laycocks," she said tensely. "If it were not so greatly against their beliefs I would wish revenge for the Laycocks."

"As to that," he hesitated and then said brusquely, "no doubt they have gone to their Quaker heaven. You'll excuse me while I go and talk to Bent. His father and mine were old friends. You'll be able to amuse yourself?"

"Yes, of course. Pray don't concern yourself about me," she said promptly, lifting her chin.

If he had hoped for some signs of reconciliation, he thrust the hope away and walked off without speaking to her again.

The camp was astir at dawn, the crier calling from group to group to wake the sluggards. The ponies had to be watered and the children fed, but the rest went fasting into the great circle. The men, their faces painted carefully, sat separate from the women, and Deborah found herself next to the round-faced Magpie.

"This is a very holy day," the girl said, patting Deborah's arm. "The Sacred Arrows will be shown to the nation."

An elderly man, clad in skins, his greased hair stuck with feathers, was dancing round the circle, arrows held up in his skinny hands. The arrows looked old and shabby, their feathered shafts frayed, but from the deep sighs that went up from the assembled Sioux it was clear that they were held in the highest honour.

There was a little silence and then the inevitable drum-beats began as a group of young braves carried in a tall cottonwood tree, its many leaved branches still green and bright. A trench had been dug in the centre of the circle and the great tree was levered upright in it and the earth stamped down.

"Now those with child will seek blessing from the Sacred Tree," Magpie said, nudging Deborah as a long line of women filed out, the meadowsweet garlands in their hands. Each garland was hung on one of the lower branches of the tree and the women left the circle as the children ran in and began to dance, even the smallest toddler imitating the com-plicated and rhythmic movements of the measure.

"You and me now," Magpie said, pulling Deborah to her feet.

"But I can't! I am a Christian," she began.

"Fleet Foot Christian too. Same Great Spirit over all," Magpie said blandly.

Deborah found herself with other young women, turning, twisting and stamping. The great tree reared above her, its flower-hung branches vibrating with life, the sunshine glinting and shimmering through the leaves. The rhythm of the drums and the wailing, piercingly sweet chanting of the women entered into her blood and bone, and she shook her bright hair free of its confining ribbon and let it coil about her shoulders.

"You will have a fine baby now," Magpie whispered breathlessly as they resumed their seats.

"A baby? Why do you say that?"

"The dance is for getting husbands and babies," Magpie said.

"Is it indeed!" Deborah raised her brows in shocked amusement, but a little thrill of pleasure ran through her at the thought of holding Adam's child in her arms.

"Now comes the Sun Dance," Magpie whispered, and in the abrupt cessation of the drumming and chanting Deborah could hear her own heart beating.

They came from the sweat lodge. Twelve young braves, naked save for brief loin-cloths, their faces painted in yellow, red and white, they ran lightly on the balls of their feet, long trails of feathers streaming from their braided hair. At the foot of the tree they flung themselves down on the ground, and men with animal skins and heads disguising their human aspects leapt into the circle, sharp knives glinting in their hands.

"Oh, no!" Deborah's cry of protest went unheard as the young men on the ground had deep slits cut in their backs and long strips of rawhide were passed beneath the flesh and tied, the free ends of the rawhide strips being fastened to the branches of the tree.

The drums began again and the young men rose and began a whirling leaping dance, their eyes half-closed, blood running in streams down to the ground.

"They dance until the skin tears loose," Magpie said, "they dance down the power of the Sun. Come! we go feast now. Buffalo steaks and fruit too! Nobody go empty today."

"I don't think I feel very hungry," Deborah said faintly. In fact she felt slightly sick and dizzy. Pushing her way through the laughing, chattering crowd she reached the river bank and knelt to splash water on her face.

"The ceremony shocked you." Adam knelt at her side, his arm about her shoulders.

"It was so – savage," she excused herself.

"In Santa Fe the Catholic Indians whip themselves and push spikes into their hands to pay honour to Christ," he told her. "The deed is mistaken, but the motive is sincere. These braves are honoured for their courage. We must honour them too."

"I am a great coward," she said miserably.

"A coward? Not you!" he exclaimed. "Many Indian women turn a little faint when they see the Sun Dance. Come! we will join the others and eat! This is a great celebration, and we must play our part as guests."

He was right, of course, but she kept her eyes resolutely turned away from the dancing, bleeding warriors as he led her to where the food was being shared out.

Fleet Foot was there, perched on a rug at her father's side. She had not danced with the other maidens, but Spotted Tail spoke eagerly as they came up. "My daughter is full of strength today. The sun warms her into health."

"Into beauty too," Adam said, squatting down. "If I didn't have a wife already I'd be tempted to ask for her."

"One of my young men has already asked if your own woman is for sale," Spotted Tail said, grinning.

"These young men think too much of themselves," Fleet Foot said, gently reproving. "Because they dance the Sun Dance they strut about like peacocks!"

"The young men are not what they were," one grizzled old Sioux declared, shaking his head. "In my youth they thought nothing of dancing the Sun Dance and hunting the buffalo the next day. Now they lie abed, groaning because of a little pain. It is the corruption of the white man that makes it so."

"I think we should make friends with the white man," Spotted Tail said. "We should smoke the peace pipe with them. Daughter, tell Laughing Flame how the first pipe came to us."

Fleet Foot gave her father the tolerant look of one who is asked to repeat a story often, folded her narrow hands, and began. "Long, long ago two men went to hunt for bison, and saw coming towards them a beautiful girl clad all in white buckskin with a golden cloud all about her. And the girl sang as she came." Fleet Foot drew a deep breath and her clear voice soared up.

"With visible breath I am walking,
A voice I send as I'm walking,
In a sacred way I am walking,
With visible tracks I am walking,
In a sacred manner I walk."

The echo of her song lingered on the air for a moment, and then Fleet Foot resumed her tale.

"As the maiden sang a sweet-scented white cloud came out of her mouth and then she gave to one of the men a pipe with twelve eagle feathers tied to the stem, and said to him 'With this you shall multiply and be a great nation.' And as they watched a golden cloud covered her, and out of the cloud there galloped a pure white bison. But the pipe remained."

"That is a beautiful tale," Deborah said softly.

"Black Kettle of the Cheyennes and Neva of the Arapahos will go in a few days to smoke pipes with Tall Chief Wynkoop," Adam said.

"And I will smoke a pipe with the Laramie pony soldier when a treaty has been agreed," Spotted Tail said. "Will Manuelito do the same?"

"We hoped to meet them here," Adam frowned. "Manuelito and Barboncito were due to attend the Sun Dance."

"They will come." It was Fleet Foot who spoke. "I feel them coming now."

"My daughter has sharp ears," Spotted Tail said proudly.

"And she's right!" Adam leapt up, shading his eyes with his hand as he peered across the wide valley. "I see them on the skyline now! Deborah, come!" He pulled her to her feet and together they ran across the clearing.

Manuelito, thinner than when they had last seen him, sprang from his horse to grip Adam's hand while Juanita, who looked tired after the journey, embraced Deborah.

"We had difficulty avoiding the pony soldier patrols," she said. "Barboncito is captured. He went back to the Canyon de Chelly to see if anything was left there, and the soldiers were waiting. But those who ride with Manuelito are safe. You look rich, Laughing Flame! Did you find gold among the Chiricahua?"

"The dress was a gift," Deborah said. "It's good to see you again, Juanita."

"And to see you. But we will talk Navajo, or have you forgotten it?"

"Nino keeps me working at it and I am teaching him to write," Deborah said proudly.

"And where is Yellow Bird?" Juanita looked about her.

"She's at Fort Wingate. It's a long story but she's quite safe. Oh, Juanita, there is so much to tell you!"

"And many days of feasting to come. We will hunt and fish and dance and be happy again," Juanita said.

The drumming had begun again. Small groups of people were chanting and dancing, following the movements of the young braves still tied to the rawhide strips. Beneath the trees the old settled themselves for a nap. The children were everywhere like flies, the little boys counting coup with long blades of spear-grass, the girls playing cats' cradle or nursing their little wooden dolls. The sun blazed down and the faint breeze was honeyscented.

"Everything is well, between you and Adam?" Juanita asked, a slight frown between her eyes.

"Everything is well," Deborah said briefly, and turned her own eyes away.

CHAPTER
EIGHT

THE Sun Dance was over, vanished into the past as if it had never been. There were times during the long winter when Deborah felt she must have dreamed the singing and the laughter. They had been on the move for half a year, never staying more than a few weeks in one place lest the patrols find them, enduring as best they could the constant blizzards that swept across the passes. Yet, incredibly, their spirits were high. Deborah, watching one of Juanita's small children manfully chewing palmilla root, choked back her own grumbles at the monotonous, inadequate diet.

Under cover of the snow and storms they had edged southward again, and were camped now high above the trading post at Zuni. It was an almost impregnable position, reached by a narrow gully that wound steeply between towering cliffs. Within the canyon was fresh water, and before the snows came there had been grass. Far below the trail led to Zuni, with its adobes of clay and stone and the big logwood cabin where goods were bartered. From time to time Adam and Deborah would risk a visit to Zuni to trade skins, and the gold earhoops that the Navajos wore, for supplies of flour and coffee. The Hopis and Zunis who lived at the post watched the tall half-breed and his red-haired companion incuriously when they rode in. Manuelito stayed up in the hill camp, venturing out only to hunt, but ammunition and arrows were becoming increasingly scarce. They had acquired a few sheep and were trying to breed from them, but it would take time to build up their stocks, and travelling down to the lower pastures so that the animals could graze was risky.

"You'd think that General Carleton would leave us alone," Deborah complained, as she and Adam rode into Zuni one day.

"Carleton is as stubborn as Manuelito, and with less reason," Adam said gloomily. "The government has ordered him to get the Navajos to the Bosque Redondo and he's determined to do exactly that."

"But we do no harm," Nino said. He was riding with them, and now drew level, his dark eyes earnest. "The pony soldiers should leave us in peace. We don't take scalps and we only raid cattle when we don't have any of our own."

"That argument counts for nothing with men like Carleton." Adam spoke curtly, but Deborah knew that his anger was not against the young brave but against the stupidity of officials who could not understand that Indians were people too.

They dismounted at the trading store, hitched their ponies to the rail, and went in. The dusty interior, its floor space taken up largely by barrels of flour, salt and gunpowder, its shelves crammed with rolls of material, coils of rope, bottles of patent medicines, boxes of nails and screws, its ceiling hung with bunches of herbs and long strings of onions, was crowded as usual with a motley collection of individuals. Several Hopis, wrapped in brightly patterned blankets, were haggling over the price of some tobacco. A couple of trappers were trying to persuade Old Tom who ran the store that they had paid too much for a gallon of whisky. In one corner a Zuni squaw was staring in bewilderment at a whalebone hoop that held out the skirts of a cambric petticoat.

Young Tom, so called to distinguish him from his father, came round to shake hands, his broad face beaming. "You came in to celebrate," he enquired.

"Celebrate what?" Adam asked blankly.

"You ain't heard? Lee signed the Confederate surrender," Young Tom said.

"You mean the war's over?"

"Been over for months bar the shouting," Young Tom said. "South's beat to its knees."

"Which means that more paupers will be pushing westward to make their fortunes," Adam said wryly, "and more soldiers will be released to fight against the Indians. What's to celebrate?"

"Some news that'll interest you more," Old Tom put in, leaning across the counter. "An old friend of yours is due in today. Had word from the Indian agent at Albuquerque."

"Which old friend?" Adam demanded.

"Herrero Grande," the trader said. "He's coming over to talk sense to Manuelito. You'd best tell your chief to come into Zuni."

"I'll think about it," Adam evaded, "if I ever run into him."

"Hell's bells! Everybody knows that he and his family are dug in hereabouts," Old Tom exclaimed. "The soldiers 'll flush 'em out, come spring, but if Herrero Grande can talk him into coming peaceable—"

"I'll meet Herrero Grande myself," Adam said. "For all we know he may be used as a Judas goat. Nino, you may ride back with Laughing Flame. I'll wait here to find out what's going on. Nino?"

He raised his voice slightly, for the young brave was staring through the open door with an expression on his face of complete stupefaction.

"Nino, what is it?" Deborah stepped to his side, following his gaze.

A wagon had drawn up outside the store and an officer, resplendent in scarlet jacket faced with gold braid, was helping a young woman to alight. The young lady was clad fashionably in a velvet travelling-dress, cuffed and collared in sable, fair hair puffed out under the wings of a velvet bonnet.

"Charity! *Charity!*" Filled with excited astonishment, Deborah flung her arms about the younger girl, hugging her tightly.

"Debbie?" Charity drew back a little, staring at her friend.

"I thought you must be dead by now – killed by the Apaches or frozen to death. We had nothing but rumours at Fort Wingate."

"A year! Lord, but it's been a whole year and there's so much to tell! Adam! Adam, ask Old Tom if we can go into the back room to talk." Deborah gabbling a little in her excitement.

"Come through. He'll not mind." Adam stood aside to allow Charity and Deborah, the red-coated officer following, to pass.

The back room, which served the storekeepers as general living quarters, was warmed by a cheerful fire. Once within Deborah seized Charity's hands, her face lively with pleasure, her words tumbling out.

"To see you again! So much has happened since we left you at the trading post with Joe. I hardly know where to begin. We went to the Sun Dance and since then we have moved about from place to place, living as best we can. Oh, but you look so pretty! Where did you get such a lovely dress, and how did you know we were coming into Zuni?"

"Give her the chance to speak!" Adam protested, laughing. "Here is Nino, you see, grown into a fine young man."

"I have been teaching him to write," Deborah said. "Nino, don't stand there with your mouth gaping like a fish!"

"I have earned both horse and fur," the boy said. "Often I wished to come, but Adam said to wait until the time was full, but now you come to me and the waiting is done."

"Debbie, you haven't met Captain Raoul Lamartine," Charity interrupted. "Adam?"

"Happy to meet you, sir." Adam shook hands politely.

"Raoul is my husband," said Charity. There was a little silence into which Deborah's voice fell like a small stone.

"Husband? Did you say—"

"A month ago," Charity said, twisting her hands together. "Raoul has an estate in Mexico. We are on our way south now – to the ranch."

"Husband? But—" Deborah could only repeat herself helplessly.

"It's been a whole year," Charity said. "I thought you gone or dead. The Navajos who came into the fort knew very little about what was happening. There was so much confusion, and I was sick. I was sick for quite a long time! The soldiers were very good to me, very kind, and Raoul was – he has been most attentive. His mother was Spanish, which is why he inherited the land in Mexico."

She stopped, flushing a little and biting her lip, dropping her eyes as Nino took a step forward. "I put my life between your hands," he said. "You are my woman promised. It was decided."

"What goes on in this place?" Raoul Lamartine demanded, entering the conversation for the first time. "*Ma belle*, what does this Indian mean?"

"I can bring you a horse now," Nino said. "A fur too. I am strong and one summer older. We said to wait two summers, Yellow Bird. I waited. I did not dance with the other maids. I am very clever at the speaking of the white man's tongue now. And I can make your name with a stick in the sand. Signs as big as a man, Yellow Bird!"

"I do not understand," Raoul Lamartine said in bewilderment. "It is most strange to me, this talk."

"I waited," Nino said. "I spoke with straight tongue to you, Yellow Bird. We made pledge."

"I thought you all dead," Charity repeated.

"But two summers are not past," Nino said. "You did not wait."

"Sir, will you have the goodness to tell me what is the meaning of all this?" Charity's husband asked.

"Nino took a fancy to me," Charity said in a high, brittle voice. "There was nothing, absolutely nothing between us! I was polite to him, no more than that, but he took it into his head to want me as his squaw. Some of these Indians do, you know, but I never gave him the slightest encouragement, I promise you!"

"Is that the truth?" The Captain, hand on his sword hilt, turned upon Nino.

The boy's eyes, as tormented as the eyes of an animal in a snare, swept over Charity from head to foot. His voice was coldly contemptuous as any aristocrat addressing a peasant. "She has spoken," he said and turned and went out without looking at any of them.

"Debbie?" Charity, her blue eyes troubled, turned to her. "You are not angry at my marriage, are you? I was all alone and Raoul is so charming. You do understand?"

"Yes. Yes, I understand." Deborah spoke sadly.

"Why don't you come with us?" Charity asked, eagerness creeping into her voice. "The ranch is a very big one and I'm so young a wife, so inexperienced, that I shall need a duenna. Do come, Debbie!"

"Our roads lie separate," Deborah said.

"But what will happen to you if you stay here?" Charity asked, her lip trembling. "There is no hope of you being left alone, you know. At the fort they are only biding their time, and there are soldiers hidden all about in the passes, waiting for Manuelito to come into Zuni."

"Are there indeed?" Adam's voice was soft, but his eyes glittered.

"*Ma chère*, that is secret!" her husband expostulated.

"Well, I never could understand these military matters," Charity pouted. "Debbie, there is a home waiting for you. Raoul would be delighted if you came with us, wouldn't you?"

"*Enchanté*," he said at once, a faintly alarmed look on his good-looking face.

"My place is with Adam," Deborah said. "I have chosen my way as you have chosen yours."

"The Navajo way? Oh, Debbie, are you sure? The life is so hard and so uncertain, even at the best of times. Wouldn't you like a comfortable bed and a dress with a hoop-skirt, and food cooked by a servant and a garden to walk in?" Charity cried.

There had been times when Deborah's bones had ached for a comfortable bed, days when she had chewed palmilla root pretending it was chicken, but now she raised her head, sending Adam a challenging glance as she said, "We will all have those things one day, but Adam and I will have them together. I do wish you happiness in your marriage."

"And you will visit us when times are more settled. It's a big ranch, the Casa Rosa, near Sonora. I haven't seen it yet, of course, but the Lamartines are a most elegant family. You will come?"

"One day," Deborah said gently, and knew that she never would. In one short year the Charity she knew had grown into this elegant young lady who wanted to be rich.

"We've no more time to waste here," Adam said. His voice was cool, his strong features set in lines of displeasure.

"You do understand?" Charity said to Deborah, the knowledge of her own treachery in her eyes.

"Yes. Captain Lamartine." Deborah held out her hand and he kissed it with such enthusiasm that she suspected he was overcome with relief at her refusal to live with them.

"Come, Laughing Flame." Adam used her Indian name as he took her arm. She gave one final glance at Charity in her fur-trimmed velvet dress and went out through the crowded store, into the snowy enclosure beyond. Nino was already mounted on his pony and under his red headknot his face was the face of a carven statue, infinitely remote.

"Go back to camp and tell Manuelito I will bring Herrero Grande to him at Ojo Caliente," Adam instructed.

"The soldiers—"

"Will be too busy guarding the passes to Zuni, and the day has not yet dawned when I cannot avoid the military. Up with you!" Adam slapped her mockingly on the rump as he hoisted her to the pony's broad back.

She and Nino rode in silence, their looks bent on the snow covered ground where the horses' hooves crunched in the tingling air. As they neared the camp she ventured to say, "You must try to understand," but he stared ahead, his voice chilled as the ice, replying, "I put my life in her hands and she let it fall."

Much later that night, huddled for warmth between Blackbird and one of Juanita's daughters, she heard his voice raised in the high wailing song of grief, but in the morning he seemed himself again as he piled the few remaining logs of wood for the fire. Only his eyes, meeting hers in a fleeting glance, shocked her with their empty despair.

Manuelito, with half-a-dozen of his braves, had slipped away to the meeting and it was three days before he rode back, Adam at his side. Both men looked grimly determined, their brows furrowed.

"Herrero Grande knew nothing of the waiting soldiers," Adam told her, as soon as they were alone, "but he is a broken reed, an echo for General Carleton."

"Then we are the only ones left?"

"Barboncito has escaped," he said, his grin triumphant. "He is back with the Chiricahua somewhere along the Little Colorado. Not all the chiefs have bowed the knee to Washington!"

"And those at the Bosque Redondo?" she asked.

"They are still there," he said briefly.

"And the conditions there?"

"Who knows? So many different tales filter out. Herrero Grande told Manuelito that the Government has promised more aid, but he has no definite information. It's months since he was on the reservation, and I, for one, would place no reliance on his word. He has been seduced by Carleton's fair words and forgotten the meaning of freedom."

"Will the soldiers attack us here?" Deborah asked nervously.

"Not while the snow lies deep and when spring comes we'll have moved on again."

"Always moving," she said on a little sigh.

"Did you feel tempted by Charity's invitation to act as her duenna?" Adam asked. His voice was teasing, but there was something in his face that made her say quickly,

"My place is with you."

"Matters have not been good between us for a long time," he said sombrely. "I wouldn't blame you if you chose to leave. That day, in the camp of the Chiricahua, I spoke in anger."

It was the nearest to an apology he was ever likely to make, but her own pent-up longing leaped to meet his questioning look, and putting her hand out towards him, she looked up into the strong planes of his face, the long lashes lying thickly above the broad, high cheekbones, the long nose and wide Irish mouth. Two races blended in this man, but she sensed that he would carve out his own destiny.

His image was blotted out as his lips pressed upon hers and the cold and hunger was a thing of no importance compared to the desire that surged through her veins. His hands moved to her bodice, unlacing it, letting it slide down over her bare shoulders. The cold air bit at her flesh but she stood motionless, eyes half closed as he undid the waistband of her short skirt and freed her limbs from the buckskin trousers beneath, until she was naked and waiting, lips parted, as he pulled off his own garments and came, warm-fleshed, to draw her down into his own male darkness. They made love as if there were no others penned in the narrow canyon, as if the world was theirs alone and the words "danger" and "unhappiness" had never even been invented.

At dawn Deborah woke, aware that Adam had moved away from her, and was crouched near the entrance of the lean-to hut where they slept.

"What is it? Why are you up?" She leaned on her elbow, pulling the blankets higher about her.

"I have not slept," he said, without turning his head.

"Are you sick?" Deborah enquired anxiously.

"Not sick, but troubled in my mind," he said sombrely.

"About the soldiers and Herrero Grande?"''

"Herrero Grande has listened to soft words and been deceived by them. Now he speaks as General Carleton wishes him to speak," Adam said impatiently. "He has no recent knowledge of conditions on the reservation, and all we have heard is that troops have been posted around to stop any Navajos from getting out."

"So?" She sat up, watching the slump of his shoulders, the thick hair that fell like rain about the strong column of his neck.

"After we met with Herrero Grande we rode back here under cover of darkness," Adam said. "Manuelito is a great man and a stubborn one, but he is a realistic one. There are fewer than a hundred of us here and another few dozen with Barboncito. But we are holding out. That is something we must make certain those on the reservation understand. We must get word to them that we are not all like Herrero Grande."

"How?"

"We discussed it," Adam said and shifted to face her. "Manuelito cannot spare one able-bodied man or woman. Anyway, if an Indian went he might find it impossible to return."

"You want me to go," she said slowly. "That's what Manuelito and you discussed, wasn't it? You want me to go to the Bosque Redondo."

"You are white and can move freely. You could present yourself as a missionary."

"A missionary! But I'm nothing of the—"

"The words are not important," he said impatiently. "What matters is that you can go to the reservation and leave it when you choose."

"If I cut your hair you could pass for Spanish," she said desperately.

"I am needed here," he said.

"And I am to be sent away? Is that why you made love to me last night?" she asked harshly.

"I made love to you because you are my woman," he said, coming back to her side, his hands reaching to pull her against him. "It needs no threat of separation to make me possess you. It has been too long."

"But you are sending me away," she said, turning her cheek away from his kiss. "How far away *is* the Bosque Redondo?"

"About three hundred miles."

"It might as well be three thousand! How long am I supposed to stay there, and when I leave, how will I ever find you again?"

"It will take you about a month to travel there in this weather," he calculated, "stay for a month – in three months we will meet at Zuni. In the Moon of Shedding Ponies."

"But I cannot ride alone!"

"Nino will go with you. It will occupy his mind, and I'll send word to the Chiricahua that you need escort."

"I can see them believing I'm a missionary," she said dryly, "if I turn up at the gates of the reservation clad in buckskins and with a horde of Apaches yelling around me."

"We will buy you a dress down at the store and some paper."

"Paper?"

"So that you can arrive with an official letter of recommendation from the Reverend Arthur Clark."

"The Reverend Arthur Clark being you, I suppose!"

"And a very worthy old gentleman he is," Adam said solemnly. "He has been most impressed by your work among the Apaches, and now sends you to the Navajos."

"You make it sound like a game," Deborah accused.

"Because that is the only way to hold back heartbreak," Adam answered, his face growing sombre. "Remember that you take hope to the people. You must make them understand that all is not lost. A group of us have evaded capture and will continue to live free. Any who contrive to escape will not find themselves alone."

"You really believe there will be a good ending to all this?"

"I know it," he said firmly. "I know it as surely as I know that I love you. One day you will find out just how deeply I love you."

"But you would send me away?"

"Not send," he said quickly, "but ask you to go. For a little time only."

"Until the Moon of Shedding Ponies." She nodded, swallowing hard because a sob threatened to rise up in her throat.

"Will you do this for us?" He asked the question gravely and she answered, equally serious, her green eyes meeting his dark ones in pledge, "I will do it."

He rode down into Zuni again that day and returned with a bolt of grey cloth, needles, thread and a length of pink lace which she gave to Juanita in return for helping to make the dress.

It was strange to wear a gown again instead of the clothes of buckskin to which she had grown accustomed. Its high neck and narrow waist constricted her, and the full, ankle-length skirt hampered her walking. With her fiery hair tied back under a small bonnet she felt alien and could manage only a faint smile when Adam, surveying her, remarked, "Now you are truly a credit to the Reverend Arthur Clark!"

"I feel all wrong!" She shifted her shoulders irritably.

"You look lovely." He kissed the tip of her nose and carefully buckled a small leather pouch about her slender waist. "There are some coins in there for urgent needs, but Manuelito is allowing you to take a pack horse with supplies for the journey, and the Chiricahua will ride with you part of the way. It is out of their territory, but their presence will deter any who seek to molest you, and Nino will carry ammunition."

"You make it sound like a day's outing," she said wryly.

"Only because there is no sense in worrying about disasters that will probably never happen. You have the mark of the survivor engraved on your nature, my love. I knew it when we first met."

"I wish I could be as certain," she said ruefully. "I can think only of the long miles growing between us and the endless days when I won't know where you are or what you're doing."

"I am a survivor too," he said, and they clung together briefly, their lips silent because there was no more to say.

"So you are ready to go." Juanita came forward as they emerged from the hut. "We will not wish you goodbye, for among friends there is no such word. The days will pass quickly for you carry a message of hope."

"Tell them that we are moving up to the San Juan to join Barboncito," Manuelito instructed. "Any who join us will help to swell our numbers. When we are many again we will return to the Canyon de Chelly and hold it against all comers. Make them understand that."

Deborah nodded obediently, smiling after the Navajo custom at leavetaking. Adam, his face inscrutable, helped her to her pony where she clung awkwardly for a moment, her full skirts rucked up.

"You have the letter and Nino will take care of you," he said, and stepped back, raising his hand.

For a moment she was tempted to cry out that she had changed her mind. The distance was too great, the time too long, the adventure too uncertain. She was only nineteen years old and still a coward who wanted the safety of her husband's arms, not this long ride across a snowy landscape. Anything might happen before she saw Adam again. She might fall sick or be taken by Mexicans or killed by renegades. Manuelito and his little band of companions might themselves be killed or captured.

"Go now," said Adam, and he spoke tightly, anguish held in check. She nodded, took the reins and trotted through the narrow clearing, past the women huddled in their shawls and the wide-eyed children. Nino followed, leading the pack pony. The young man scarcely spoke these days save when he was directly addressed, and then he answered mechanically, as if his mind were far across the Mexican border with Charity in her velvet gown.

At the bend in the rocks where the clearing narrowed into a gully Deborah turned, raising her hand, and saw Adam, a black figure against the whiteness of the snow, looking after her.

CHAPTER
NINE

"Miss Deborah Jones, you say?" The young Army officer scratched his fair head and peered suspiciously at the girl before him.

She was clad, respectably enough, in a travel-stained grey gown under a buffalo cloak, and her hair was scraped back demurely under a small bonnet. Red hair, he noted, and the girl herself was no beauty, being small and scrawny with a nose that turned up at the end and a mouth too wide for fashionable taste. Then she lifted huge, greenish eyes and he blinked, wondering why he had thought her plain.

"I have a letter of authorisation, sir, from the Reverend Arthur Clark," she said.

"Your uncle, you say?"

"Yes, Captain—?" She put her head on one side questioningly.

"Paul, ma'am. Paul Sinclair."

"You have an English accent," she said.

"Boston, ma'am, but my parents came from the Old Country."

"My own parents were English," she said sweetly. "After they died my uncle brought me up."

"And he's a minister, you say?"

"Yes sir, converting the Apaches, but it's uphill work!"

"I can imagine it. Can't fathom how you managed to survive." He scratched his head again, staring past her to where the young Indian who had ridden with her up to the gates stood, holding the ponies.

"My uncle was becoming concerned by the unrest among the Chiricahua," she said demurely. "He also felt that it was time I began to preach the Word on my own account, and I have had some – experience with the Navajos. There is no missionary here at the Bosque Redondo?"

"Well, no, but there's no accommodation for a lady." His pleasant face was troubled. "My men are garrisoned at the fort, and those on guard duty use the barrack hut."

"Surely there's a store or an agency house?"

"There's a room at the back of the store," he said slowly. "That could be used, I suppose."

"Then perhaps you could have it fixed up for me."

"By rights I ought to have a word with the commander, but right now he's away at Albuquerque." The young officer was becoming more and more discomposed.

"And am I to stand out in the cold until he returns?" Deborah enquired.

"No, ma'am. Come in, do! You'll pardon the disorder? This is my working office, not intended for company." He was bustling about, moving piles of papers from one chair to the next.

"Nino, see to the horses and tell the others to expect me." Deborah spoke briskly in Navajo as she stepped within.

"You speak the language, ma'am?" Paul Sinclair exclaimed in surprise.

"Sufficient to make myself understood."

"I cannot make head or tail of it," he confessed. "Luckily some of them speak a little English or Spanish, but they're not too friendly."

"Perhaps you are not friendly towards them."

"I have my duty to do, ma'am." He helped her off with her buffalo robe and began to brew coffee over the small fire in the corner of the room.

"As I have mine." At his uncomprehending look she added virtuously, "To preach the Word."

"As you say, Miss Jones." He gave her another puzzled glance.

"There are rumours that conditions are bad here," she said.

"They're not good, ma'am," he said frankly. "The land's poor – thin soil and too many stones, and the water in the creek is bitter – brackish taste to it. The snow's melting now, which is a blessing, so we'll get some seeds planted in a week or two. We've been waiting for the delivery of farm tools, but the weather's held up supplies all along the route. The man with you is a Navajo."

"That's right."

"Knew him by his top-knot." The Captain looked pleased with himself. "They all pull their hair up into that tail, you know."

"Yes, I know."

"And the squaws wear braids. Nice-looking people, some of them. Seems a pity to pen them up here, but the Government must have its reasons, I suppose. If you'll pardon me, ma'am, I'll go and see my orderly about getting that room ready for you."

He bowed and went out. Deborah went to the window and looked out over the compound. The snow was melting, deep puddles filmed with ice lying on the uneven ground. There were neither trees nor shrubs, only a cluster of mud hogans and a couple of soldiers patrolling in the distance. There was none of the usual cheerful bustle that she had grown to expect in an Indian camp.

"Laughing Flame, this is a bad place." Nino had returned and crossed the room to join her. "No tools for planting. Not allowed to hunt. Bad water that makes children sick! Not a good place!"

"You've seen the others?"

"They say Star Chief Carleton told many bad lies to them. Made many false promises, and now the soldiers stop them from leaving. They keep counting people and writing things down in books. What good is writing down things in books when there is nothing to eat?"

He sounded angry and bewildered, but at least the blank, unseeing look had gone from his eyes. Deborah put her hand on his arm, her voice soothing. "It does look very bad, Nino, but at least we are here and can try to help. We must make them understand that Manuelito is holding out and will not surrender."

"There are many dying," he said. "New sicknesses, brought by the white man. They cough and sneeze and shiver and then they lay down and die."

"Is that true, Captain Sinclair?" Deborah turned as the officer came back into the room.

"Ma'am?"

"Is it true that the death rate is high?"

"I fear so," he admitted. "Nearly a thousand have died, and the thaw will bring more sickness. They don't seem to have much resistance to infection."

"Surely something can be done."

"We're waiting for medical supplies," he assured her. "To tell the truth, Miss Jones, I'm posted to Fort Laramie at the end of the month, and I won't be sorry to leave. This is a Godforsaken place!"

"But good enough for Indians," she flashed.

"Ma'am, I do what I can to make matters better for them," Captain Sinclair said, his manner frosting visibly.

"Yes, of course." She gave him a quick, mollifying smile.

"And it's no picnic for my men," he continued. "They get very bored stuck out in this wilderness, with nothing to do but take tallies."

"It must be very difficult." She gave him a warmly sympathetic look.

"Yes, ma'am, and there's very few appreciate my problems. The Indians won't co-operate! They stand in line demanding beef rations when I've not enough for my own men. I got them a few Army tents on my own authority, and they coolly informed me they'd 'do' until we got wood for houses. Nobody ever told me that Indians lived in houses!"

"Many of them do," Deborah said, amused despite herself. "They take tepees with them on hunting parties or if they're visiting other tribes."

"Well, it'll be a big relief when I get back to Fort

Laramie," he said. "Now if you'll accompany me, ma'am, I'll show you to your quarters, and I apologise right this minute for their makeshift quality. Fact is we're just not ready to receive ladies, and I don't know how I'm going to contrive a guard for you. We're short as it is with three of my men down with dysentery – begging your pardon!"

"Nino is my bodyguard." Deborah smiled at the captain. "I will settle in and take a look round if I may."

"And you will join me for supper, I hope?"

"Indeed I will, sir." She smiled at him again, knowing that she might need an ally if she were ever to give any help to those at the Bosque Redondo.

In the days that followed she quickly realised that conditions were very bad indeed. The bleak and treeless site was swept continually by a bitter east wind against which there was no protection. The crude hogans and few tents were adequate for only the more privileged, most of the families having had to dig shelters for themselves out of the ground, covering them with rush mats. Wherever she looked there were children, weeping with cold and fretful from hunger, squaws huddled within the threadbare blankets, braves whose sullen, haggard looks were in unhappy contrast to the vigour and courage of the people she had known.

"They lied to us, Laughing Flame," Armijo said. "We were promised good land to plant and sheep to raise, and leave to hunt if food was scarce. It was all false! There is no grain and few sheep, not even wood for the building of houses! And they will not let us leave the reservation in order to hunt."

"Manuelito and Barboncito are holding out," she told him earnestly.

"But for how long? The Apaches cannot feed them for ever and the pony soldiers are everywhere now that the war between north and south is over."

"They want us to die," another said gloomily. "The white man is to inherit the earth and the red man is to die out. They call it Manifest Destiny."

"Have many left the reservation?" Deborah enquired.

"A few, but it is not easy to slip past the guards," Armijo said. "Even if we do evade them, how are we to reach our land without horses or supplies?"

"I will speak to the captain," Deborah promised, rising from the squatting position in which she was seated.

"It is not the captain but Star Chief Carleton who should be brought here to see conditions," Armijo said, his expression sombre. "The captain is a fool, but he does what he can."

"Armijo is not a bad man," Captain Sinclair said later. "He's ignorant and uneducated, of course, but I've found nothing savage or cruel in him. It's unfortunate that he has no conception of the wider issues involved."

"Manifest Destiny?" She arched her eyebrows enquiringly.

"Yes, ma'am. It is the manifest destiny of the red man to yield to the white."

"And you believe that?"

"I'm sorry about it, ma'am, but facts are facts." He poured more coffee for them both. "The railroads are pushing westward and the telegraph lines will soon stretch from end to end of the country. There are new gold strikes out in California, a new silver strike in Nevada! Progress, ma'am, and these natives are holding it back. They attack the railroad coaches, climb up the telegraph poles and cut the wires, and they have no notion of the value of money!"

"So they are to be starved and frozen to death on barren land, are they?"

"No, ma'am, that I don't believe!" he said vehemently. "We ought to take good care of these folks. They're like children, you see. Always on about the Great Spirit and various totems and taboos. Mere children!"

Deborah hid a smile, thinking of the elaborate social structure by which the Indians lived. In all her months with them she had never seen an old person neglected or a child unjustly beaten.

"I'm sure you do your best, sir," she said aloud.

"As you do, ma'am, but it's of little use trying to persuade them to a Christian way of thinking."

"You're probably right, but one must try." She folded her hands demurely. "It will be Eastertide soon, and there should be some sort of feast to mark it. Is it possible for some meat to be bought?"

"Supplies are due, ma'am, but they're usually late and I have to see to the needs of my own men first."

"Cannot leave of absence be given to some of the young men so they could hunt?"

"The Navajos are not supposed to leave the reservation."

"But if you spoke to the commander at Fort Sumner then he might waive the rule."

"Miss Jones, army regulations were not made to be waived!" the captain said, looking faintly shocked. "If we give those young bucks horses and weapons and turn them loose, that's the last we'll see of them. They'll head westward to join their chiefs and then my head will be on the block at headquarters."

"If they give their word—"

"They'd only break it. Bless you, Miss Jones," he said, looking amused, "but they don't understand the importance of keeping one's word. They cannot even be persuaded to put their mark to a written agreement."

"Life must be very difficult for you," she said.

"I do my duty, ma'am, but I'll not be sorry to get back to Fort Laramie. There is much more social life there."

"When do you leave?"

"Day after tomorrow. Fact is that I'll leave with only one regret."

"Oh?" She glanced at him in question.

"I don't like having to leave you, ma'am. Oh, I know you feel you have a mission, but this is a lonely place for a female, and it's clear you were gently reared. Now, if you wished for more congenial surroundings, I would be happy to recommend you personally to Colonel Maynadier."

"That's very kind of you, but—"

"Think about it. Don't answer it now," he said, raising his hand. "I would take it as a personal favour if you did decide to accept my escort up to Fort Laramie. There's be more company for you up north."

"You're very kind." Deborah smiled at him with genuine liking, wondering why his wavy fair hair and steady grey eyes had no power to move her emotionally when the mere thought of Adam sent a quiver of desire through her. She had been almost two weeks at the Bosque Redondo and there had been more than a month's travelling before that. She had never woken without his image in her mind, nor fallen asleep without trying to pretend that his arms enfolded her.

"I'll leave a requisition for more meat," he said, "though I doubt if anything much will come of it. Word from the south is bad. Plantations destroyed, thousands of people dispossessed – it's a sad business, the aftermath of war."

"Yes. Yes, it must be."

"And these are not subjects to interest a lady. I do apologise, ma'am." He rose, bowing politely as she left.

Outside Nino was waiting for her as usual. There was something of the duenna in his attitude towards her, she thought with amusement, as he straightened up from the rail against which he was leaning. "Is hunting to be allowed?" he asked.

"No. Captain Sinclair believes that rules are not intended to be bent or broken," she said wryly.

"He has no sense, that one." Nino fell into step beside her as she walked towards the store. 'Store' was no more than a euphemism for the shabby hut, its roof leaking, its shelves long since emptied of goods. The narrow room at the back with its tin washbasin and army bunk was chilly and unwelcoming, but it was infinitely better than the hovels in which the Navajos existed.

"He has no imagination," she said, going over to poke the small fire into a blaze.

"We will leave this place soon?"

"As soon as I can contrive a sufficient excuse. At least I can take back a report on conditions here. I only wish I could do something to change them!"

"You are most good," he said earnestly. "When Adam-Leap-The-Mountain first told us that he planned to marry a white woman there was some talk. Many feared a white woman would be stupid or faithless. We were glad to be wrong."

"And Yellow Bird?" Deborah ventured.

"I do not speak her name," he said with dignity. "I sang the grief song for her and now it is as if she had never lived. In a year or two, when the pain is less, I will take a wife to bear me sons and I will be good to her. That is how a man should act, isn't it?"

"Yes, Nino, it is." She gave him a look of sympathy, hoping that his eventual marriage would be less loveless than he appeared to expect.

"One of the pony soldiers is a good man," Nino informed her, changing the subject. "He is a sergeant soldier – very tall with loud voice. He will buy chickens for us, he says."

"Can you trust him?"

"The others say he talks straight and keeps his word," Nino assured her. "For two gold pieces he will bring in many chickens."

The money pouch that Adam had buckled about her waist contained, he had told her, money for necessities. She unclasped it and took out two gold pieces. "Give these to the sergeant soldier and tell him to buy chickens. At least the children will have a little meat."

"If I give him a gold coin for himself he will let some of us go hunt and not tell the Captain," Nino said.

She fished again in the pouch and took out another coin. The neck of the leather bag was narrow and as she tugged at it impatiently the cord snapped, sending a little shower of coins up in the air.

One glinted near her foot. As Nino scrambled for the rest she bent to pick it up. It clung to her hand. A hollow circle with something engraved on the inner rim. *S.L.J.L.* A heart between them, joining the two in life and death.

Sarah Laycock. John Laycock. Everything inside her screamed a denial and then she raised her eyes and saw the expression on Nino's face.

"Tell me, Nino. Tell me about it." Her voice was as thin, as papery as a dead leaf.

"Adam made us swear not to tell," the boy said. "The ring—"

"Was in the lining. It fell out as the lining tore. *Tell me!*"

"Adam wanted you for his woman."

He had asked her to go away with him on that first day by the pool, and she had refused.

"He killed them," she said, her voice shaking with horror.

"He said nobody was to tell because you would be very angry."

Not Utes thundering across the stony ground, but Navajos! A half-breed, seeking a mate, seeking revenge for his rejection.

"Were you there?" she whispered. Nino shook his head.

"The others went. They searched in the caves and saw a drawing there – a new drawing."

Charity had scratched it with a stone near to the magical hunting pictures.

"He said not to tell," the boy said again.

"He killed them?" She repeated the words helplessly, praying for some denial.

"Burned everything," Nino nodded. "He said you would be angry if you knew, but he wanted you for his woman. He wanted you very much."

She slipped the ring slowly on her finger and stared at it, remembering the Laycocks with their gentle manners, their idealism. They had been good to her, taking her in and treating her as their own daughter.

"If there is a hunt am I to go on it?" Nino asked. "I would come back after two, three sleeps. Am I to go?"

"Yes. Yes, give the sergeant the money and tell him you

are to go on the hunt." She spoke absently, scarcely aware of her words.

"Are you sick, Laughing Flame?" he enquired anxiously. "Men do sometimes kill when they want a woman. Adam—"

"I'm not sick!" If she heard once more that Adam had wanted her as his woman she would lose the last vestige of her control and begin to scream.

"Angry, then? Are you angry with me? Will you tell Adam that I told?"

"No, I'll not tell him." I'll never tell Adam anything again because, God willing, I'll never see him again in my life.

"They died quick, you know," Nino said. "He knew you would want them to die quick."

"Go to the sergeant." She spoke through gritted teeth, holding herself tense as he backed to the door.

The coins were still scattered around her feet. She knelt to pick them up, counting each one aloud to stop the thoughts from crowding into her mind. Twenty-seven gold coins and three more she had given to Nino. Thirty pieces of gold.

"They should have been silver," she said aloud and began to cry, angrily, without tears.

When she presented herself before the Captain, however, she was quite composed, her hair sleeked down, her mouth prim. "You offered to escort me to Fort Laramie, sir."

"And you promised to think about it."

"I have been thinking." She drew a deep breath and said, "Perhaps it would be wiser for me to travel north with you. I do confess that I miss female companionship."

"We leave the day after tomorrow, ma'am. Can you be ready by then?"

Nino would still be off the reservation if the sergeant was willing to be bribed, and she would be able to leave without his trying to prevent her. "Yes. I can be ready," she said bleakly.

"We will have a supply wagon," he said. "You will find it more comfortable to ride in the wagon, and I will have a bed fixed up for you inside it."

"I don't wish to be a trouble," she said tonelessly.

"The journey will be a long and difficult one," he warned, "and we are a small party. Naturally we will keep to the main trails, and the time of year should bring fine weather."

"Yes." She cared little if they never even got to the end of the journey.

"You want to send word to your uncle, ma'am?"

"My—? Oh, there's no need. He won't expect any word from me."

"Well, if you're sure." He gave her a doubtful glance, wondering what had happened to the life in her face. She had lost all her sparkle and sat now like a frozen thing, saying the correct words in a polite little voice from which all the animation had fled.

"Are you sure you're feeling well, Miss Jones?" he enquired anxiously.

"I'm a little tired," she confessed.

"And dispirited? I know the feeling, ma'am. This place takes the heart out of you."

"Yes." She broke briefly, pressing her hands together.

Her heart had been taken from her by Adam-Leap-The-Mountain, she thought. Now there was nothing inside her but a cold, empty space.

"Will you do me the honour of having supper with me tonight?" Captain Sinclair asked.

"What? Oh, no, thank you. I'm a trifle weary tonight."

"You're not sickening for anything, are you?" he asked in quick alarm.

The thaw had set in, and the thaw brought with it disease.

"I'm quite well. Just tired."

"If you'll forgive me for saying so, ma'am, the sooner we get you to more civilised parts the better pleased I'll be!" he said frankly. "I've no wish to speak against your uncle, for I've not had the pleasure of meeting him, and as you say he's a religious gentleman, but it simply isn't right to drag a pretty young lady into savage parts. You're not offended at my plain speaking?"

"No, of course not." Deborah wondered hazily exactly what he'd been saying, for his words had dropped like pebbles into the empty well of her understanding.

"If you knew how much I loved you," Adam had said.

Enough to follow and kill the Laycocks and Jed. Nino had said it, and Nino wasn't a liar, even if she had not had the evidence of the ring. Perhaps, one day, Adam would have admitted it to her, when she was so closely bound to him that there would be no sense in her trying to break free. But it was futile to think of what Adam might have intended. She had put her life between his hands and he had crushed it into his own savage design.

"My pleasure to offer you my escort," Captain Sinclair was saying.

"You're very kind, sir."

"Paul, ma'am. I would take it as a privilege if you would consent to call me by my first name. I understand that the Indians call you—"

"My name is Deborah," she said quickly.

Deborah Jones, on her way to Fort Laramie under the escort of Captain Paul Sinclair. Not Laughing Flame. Never Laughing Flame again.

CHAPTER
TEN

AT any other time Deborah would have loved the changing colours of the landscape as spring yielded to summer, but now the brilliance of the flowers that starred the grass was muted by her own misery, and the face she turned to the emerging sun was tense with unhappiness.

It was easy to tell herself that she hated Adam, but more difficult to banish the memories of the loving they had shared. In dreams he was always there, smiling down at her, calling her his woman, and then the dream would change to nightmare and she would see the tenderness in his dark face turn to savagery and his hands drip blood. More than once she had woken, sobbing, from such a nightmare to find Captain Sinclair bending over her, his pleasant face drawn into lines of uncomprehending concern as he said, "Miss Debbie! Miss Debbie, do wake!" He was unfailingly thoughtful for her comfort, often halting their small train for longer than necessary in order to give her time to rest. When they made camp at night he would join her for the inevitable jerky and beans and talk about his family in Boston.

His parents were shopkeepers and his elder brother would carry on the business. "Tim being the brains of the family! My own fancy was always for soldiering, so in a way the war was a blessing. It gave me a career."

He had two younger sisters, one married and the other still at school, and an assortment of cousins, some of whom had fought on the Union side. This western posting had given him the opportunity to travel, but he was glad to be leaving the Bosque Redondo behind and returning to the more congenial surroundings of Fort Laramie.

"Not that I expect to stay there for very long, Miss Debbie. Colonel Maynadier has indicated to me that there's every probability of my being called to Washington in the near future. That would mean promotion and a secure administrative post."

"Your family will be pleased," she said.

"Indeed they will, ma'am. My mother was never too happy about my embarking on a military life, but now there is no reason for her to fret. And it means I shall be in a position to settle and marry."

"How nice," she said vaguely.

"Not that I anticipate any great passionate involvement," he said earnestly. "I'm of a phlegmatic nature, Miss Debbie, not given to romantic fancies. A bit of a dull dog, as you might say."

"No, indeed," she said earnestly. "I find you very good company. Certainly you have made this journey most pleasant for me."

"Truly?" He flushed with pleasure. "You know, Miss Debbie, your own presence these past weeks has led me to wonder – we do seem to rub along rather well together."

"Yes, indeed."

"I don't earn a great deal as yet, but I am due for an increase in pay, and a promotion as I was telling you. I am in the position now of being able to contemplate marriage, and our being thrown together in this manner – I am not a fanciful man, but I am apt to attribute it to the workings of fate."

He was proposing to her. She realised the fact with dull surprise.

"If your own affections are not engaged—" He gazed at her hopefully.

"No, they are not," she said quickly.

"And you are not indifferent to my regard?"

The truth was that she was indifferent to everything, numb to pleasure or pain. Only in sleep was her emptiness filled by the anguish of memory. "I would be very happy to marry you," she said flatly.

"Then you do me great honour, ma'am. When we reach Fort Laramie we can—"

"Must we wait until then?" she interrupted.

When she had been a little girl with an aching tooth her father had taken her at once to the tooth-puller. "For if you delay the root will fester and cause you more pain in the end."

"Before we get to Laramie! Why, yes, there is a mission a few miles west of here. The priest there – we are not of his faith – but in these isolated parts, I'm sure he might be prevailed upon to officiate." He looked at her in bewilderment.

"Having travelled with you unchaperoned," she said, "I would feel less embarrassed if we could be married as soon as possible."

"Of course. That's a consideration I never took into account," he said.

If he thought her delicate susceptibilities at variance with her travelling only in the company of an Indian, he was too polite to say so.

"Your commander won't object?" she asked.

"Indeed not, ma'am. He will welcome you heartily," Paul Sinclair assured her. "But I had imagined you might need time to prepare."

"A quiet ceremony would suit me very well," Deborah said. "I must be frank and tell you now that I don't have any – I am not romantically inclined."

"The most enduring relationships are those built upon mutual trust and friendship," he said.

She nodded, forcing a smile as he leaned and brushed her cheek with his lips. He was kind-hearted and attractive, and in time she would grow accustomed to his pompous ways and his utter lack of imagination.

"It's getting late, ma'am. You'll excuse me if I do the rounds?" He rose from the fire, giving his usual stiff little bow.

"Is the duty sergeant sick?"

"No, Miss Debbie. Trooper Evans has a slight chill, but nothing to speak of, and the rest of the men are quite fit and well. The truth is that one or two have reported seeing Indians in the area. Now we've not seen one since we set out, and it's my own belief that the men are jumping at shadows, but to be on the safe side I'll make the rounds myself. I wouldn't fret about it if I were you. Our scouts have reported no hostiles in the area."

"I won't fret. Goodnight."

She stayed by the fire, her buffalo cloak wrapped about her, for the nights were still cool. The three supply wagons were drawn up in a line, and beyond the fire one of the troopers was strumming softly on a guitar. From somewhere in the surrounding hills a coyote called, and was answered by another. The hair at the back of her neck prickled and she found herself listening intently, but the cries were not repeated and after a little while she climbed up into the wagon and prepared for sleep.

They would pass fairly close to the Mission within a day or so. The detachment would be halted and then she and the Captain, with an escort of two or three, would ride to the ceremony. News of the engagement had been greeted with little surprise. The men congratulated her and wished her well in their laconic fashion, though she guessed some of them thought the Captain could have done better for himself. Females were in such short supply, however, that she suspected that they also envied him a little.

"When we reach Fort Laramie we'll have a wedding breakfast," Paul Sinclair said. "The ladies there will want to bake a cake and put on a little celebration. I must contrive to obtain a ring."

"This one will do. It belonged to – to a dear friend of mine," Deborah said, indicating the gold band. Looking at it strengthened her resolve. The Laycocks were dead, Charity in Mexico, her own love betrayed by violence. Marriage to Paul Sinclair offered a new opportunity, a new life, and she would be a fool to let the chance slip.

"Two or three weeks will see us in Laramie," he told her. "You're certain you don't wish to wait?"

If she waited she might begin to stir out of the peculiar numbness that had descended upon her feelings. "Are you regretting the pledge we made?" she asked lightly.

"Indeed I'm not, Miss Debbie," he said solemnly. "I shall be the happiest of men when I can introduce you as my bride. It would be perfect if my family could be present, of course. My mother always feared lest I choose what she calls 'a flighty young piece', so she will be delighted to meet you."

Deborah, aware of her plain dress and the hair scraped into submission, couldn't resist a wry smile at the back-handed compliment.

"It's a pity you cannot send word to your uncle," Paul was saying.

"My uncle? Oh, he's probably been scalped by now," she said vaguely, and aware of the Captain's astonished look, added hastily, "He is such a religious man that he quite looked forward to going to Heaven."

"Then I am only thankful that you came unscathed to the Bosque Redondo!" he exclaimed.

"Let us hope we reach Laramie unharmed," she said piously.

"I have every expectation that we will. These rumours of Indians seem to have died a natural death. Anyway, they are not likely to be hostiles with the Mission so near."

"No, of course not." She smiled at him, trying to ignore the odd little shiver of apprehension that rippled down her spine.

There had been several moments recently when she had had the distinct impression of being watched, but when she had turned to scan the horizon only the crouching shapes of bushes and trees had met her gaze.

The Mission was larger than she had expected, its walls of stone, its roof tiled and shining below them as they rode down into the wide valley. The supply wagons had been left in charge of the men and only a couple of troopers had accompanied them on the three-mile journey to the Mission.

"It is a lovely day for a wedding," she said, making her voice cheerful and interested.

The previous night she had slept little, tossing and turning in the stuffy wagon while disconnected images flashed behind her closed lids. Adam lifting one of the little ones to his shoulder and laughing. Adam bending over the pot of chicken stew and fishing out a bit of meat with his long, beautifully-shaped fingers. Mrs. Laycock, her plain face glowing into beauty, as she listened to her husband reading from his treasured copy of the Bible. Charity in her velvet dress, her fair curls bouncing on her shoulders as she spun round and round, dancing for a Commanche who stood with hatchet upraised and scalps dangling from his belt.

"I have visited the Mission only once before, but Father Purcell is a very pleasant gentleman," Paul Sinclair said. "You will like him, Miss Debbie, though he is not of the same persuasion as ourselves."

As they neared the building, several figures lounging about on the dusty track glanced up incuriously. They were Pawnees, to judge from the pattern of stripes on their faces, and she felt a sudden distaste for their oiled, half-naked bodies and plaited hair. The Pawnee were disliked by other tribes for their readiness to act as scouts for the invading whites. She had heard Manuelito talk against them many times.

The big wooden gate was open and they rode into a compound with numerous huts and tepees scattered about between the cottonwood trees. A small, plump figure, a fringe of white hair surrounding his bald patch, hurried towards them, flapping away several Pawnees who tugged at his black soutane, trying to tempt him with a large red ball.

"Get away! Get away! Shoo! Shoo! It's Captain Sinclair, isn't it? We met last year when you were on your way to the

Bosque Redondo." He had a breathless voice with a hint of Irish.

"Indeed we did. I'm glad to find you well, Father."

Paul Sinclair dismounted and shook hands.

"Nothing ever ails me," the priest said, hitching up the skirt of his habit.

"No trouble, then?"

"Trouble? Oh, *trouble*!" Father Purcell waved a dismissing hand. "Sure, but there's always trouble! We were born into the world to make troubles a mite easier for mankind. And who is the young lady?"

"Miss Deborah Jones." Paul turned to help her dismount.

"Delighted to meet you, ma'am." The priest shook hands vigorously. "You'll come in for a bite to eat? And you'll be wanting a wash and brush-up. You never rode all this way with no other escort?"

"The rest of my detachment are back with the wagons."

"Ah, then you must have special business with me. Come in, come in." He bustled the two of them towards the building, pausing to instruct the troopers. "There's a place in the stables and hay for the horses, and you'll get a bite to eat at the cook-house. Tell Concepta I sent you, and keep your thoughts on the food and not on the wench. I got her to agree to a respectable Christian baptism last week, and I've no wish to officiate at a baptism in nine months' time."

"I assure you, Father, my men have the highest morals," Paul began stiffly.

"Stuff and nonsense! Never met a soldier with morals yet," Father Purcell said. "Some of these Pawnee squaws are good-looking, eager to please, very generous. Part of my job to curb that generosity a little. What can I do for you and the young lady?"

"We wish to be married," Paul said.

"Married, is it?" The priest's eyebrows shot up, "You're not three weeks from Fort Laramie. Why not wait until then?"

"We hoped for a quiet wedding," Deborah said. "I feel – a little awkward at the idea of arriving at the fort without—" She hesitated.

"Without the dignity of the wedded state to cast into the teeth of the scandalmongers, eh? And where did you meet, then?"

"At the Bosque Redondo. I had been with my uncle preaching the Word to the Chiricahuas."

"And you still with your hair on! Where's your uncle?"

"He thought I would be safer on the reservation. I met Captain Sinclair there, and as he was returning to Fort Laramie—"

"You decided to give up missionary work and become an Army wife, eh?"

"Can you perform the ceremony?" Paul asked. "I don't need the permission of my commanding officer, but I can vouch for his approval."

"It's the Lord's approval that counts." Father Purcell moved to a cupboard in the corner of the austerely furnished room and took out a flask. "Irish whiskey," he nodded. "One of the Lord's gifts to his sinful creatures! We'll drink a tiny toast to His approval. Be so good as to pass me those three tin mugs."

Deborah did as she was bidden, and he poured a small measure into each. "Glory be to God and His Holy Mother!" Father Purcell raised his mug, then drank with relish. "So! You want to be wed, do you? You're neither of you Catholics, I take it?"

"Does it matter?" Deborah asked. The mouthful of liquor had warmed her and she was suddenly anxious to get on with the ceremony.

"Under normal circumstances and the Bishop being present, yes, it might. But these are not normal circumstances and His Lordship is unhappily absent. Now you'll be needing a special licence, and that I can draw up while you're making yourself ready. Your men can be called in as witnesses."

"I don't have a dress," Deborah began, but the priest, his skirts flying, was opening the door to an inner chamber furnished as simply as the other.

In one corner was a deep chest, its lid scored and scratched. He crossed and opened it, beckoning her within as he lifted out a white garment. "My mother's wedding dress," he said, his voice reverent. "She died when I was a lad, and I brought it with me all the way from the Old Country back in 'forty-nine. It was the time of the Hunger, and me just ordained. She'd have liked to see that."

"But I couldn't—" Deborah began.

"Time it was worn again. She'd have liked that too, especially with your hair being the same colour as hers used to be. There's water in the basin and a clean towel. You get ready now, and I'll see to the making out of the licence."

He smiled at her and went out, closing the door softly. The dress lay in a swirl of time-yellowed silk over the bed. Deborah went over and picked it up, automatically holding it against her. It had the dropped shoulder-line and ballooning sleeves of the styles fashionable forty-odd years before. Its full skirt would be a trifle long and it was a mite too wide across the bustline, but the long white sash could be pulled tightly to compensate.

For a moment longer she hesitated and then the queer feeling of urgency swept over her again, and she began to unlace the grey gown.

The water was cold enough to sting colour into her cheeks, and the dress fitted more closely than she had hoped. She pulled her hair loose from its confining ribbon and took out her comb, smoothing the long ringlets about her fingers. There was a square mirror in the room, and she gazed at her reflection with a slow dawning of pleasure. Certainly she would make a most comely bride.

And she was marrying a man for whom she had not the slightest affection. The sentence formed as clearly in her mind as if someone had just spoken it aloud.

She had no more business to be wedding Captain Paul

Sinclair than she had to be wearing a dress that had belonged to an Irish woman long since laid to rest beneath the green turf of her homeland.

A tap on the door, and Father Purcell stood on the threshold, his small eyes twinkling. "Now don't you look like the blessed St. Brigid herself!" he exclaimed. "There's good Irish blood in you somewhere, I'll be bound!"

"Father, I—" Deborah opened her mouth to protest, to explain that she had made a dreadful mistake, that she intended to spend the rest of her life as a spinster.

"My mother will be dancing a jig up among the holy saints to see you looking so fine!" the priest rushed on. "The licence is ready to be signed, so we'll go into the church for the ceremony. I've sent young José to get your troopers to act as witnesses, and I've no doubt at all that some of the squaws will be coming in to watch. All the ladies love a wedding! Now, Captain Sinclair, how do you like your bride?"

"You look charming, Miss Debbie," Paul said, offering his arm with a little bow.

It was wrong. Everything was all wrong. She wanted to cry out her protest, but Father Purcell was opening a side door and ushering them into the cool, whitewashed interior of a church, its altar lit by six tall white candles set in silver sconces, a few stools and benches providing seating accommodation for the congregation.

"If you will stand here." Father Purcell indicated a spot below the raised step of the altar.

But this smartly-dressed young officer, his fair hair sleeked down, was a stranger. She had no feelings for him at all, and she doubted if anything more than kindness had prompted his offer of marriage. It had been a terrible mistake, but when she tried to speak her throat closed up and she could only smile, like a foolish-faced rag doll she had seen once sat in the front window of a store in Kansas City.

"You both understand that matrimony is a sacrament?" Father Purcell said, facing them. "It is a solemn vow made between a man and a woman in the presence of Almighty God that they will cleave together as one flesh for the procreation of children and for the mutual comfort and pleasure of the two parties. You do understand that?"

"Yes, Father." It was Paul who spoke, his voice firm and clear.

Deborah nodded, her eyes wide on the priest's face. In a moment something inside her would break loose and begin screaming, and once that started she feared it would never stop.

"You are both of you free to wed?" Father Purcell's voice held a hint of mild jocularity.

"Quite free," Paul said, and Deborah found herself nodding again, up and down, up and down, like a mechanical toy whose mechanism had broken.

"Your witnesses are here," Father Purcell said, smiling past them towards the main door.

The smile stayed on his lips, froze there, petrified into a grimace. The padding of moccasined feet thudded on the stone louder than boots. Deborah turned, very slowly as if she were still on strings, and saw them, oiled and pointed with scalplocks braided and stuck with feathers.

There must have been about fifty Commanches, seeming to have risen up out of her own most lurid imaginings. The scream bubbled into her throat and stayed there as a tall figure strode through them to her side.

Adam was all Navajo today, with nothing in him of his Irish mother. His face was painted in stripes of yellow and white, and he wore the buckskin shirt and trousers worn by most of the braves. His black hair was drawn up into a tail at the crown of his head and secured with a scarlet cloth, and in his hands he held a long hunting rifle. His eyes, fixed upon her, were ablaze with contempt.

"So, you decided on a Christian ceremony?" He spoke bitingly, his lips curled into a sneer.

"Adam." The word emerged, not as a scream, but flat and toneless as if it had no meaning.

"Is this the gentleman whom you planned to wed?" He turned to eye Paul Sinclair. "He's a pretty fellow, nearly as pretty as Charity's French dandy."

"My troopers—" Paul began, his lips whitening.

"Hit over the head with their own rifles and securely tied up. Your tame Pawnees are hiding in the cookhouse, Father. No harm will come to them, unless, of course, you refuse to perform the ceremony."

"Ceremony?" Deborah's voice cracked with strain.

"The wedding ceremony between Deborah Jones and Adam-Leap-The-Mountain," he said.

"Deb— do you *know* this man?" Paul demanded.

"She knows me – intimately," Adam drawled.

"And hates you." Deborah found her voice and spoke loudly. "I left the Bosque Redondo—"

"So Nino told me when he rode back to Zuni. It was sheer chance that he found me there. I'd risked going in for supplies. As it was it took me weeks to pick up your trail."

"You were following us," she said bleakly.

"Right to the altar," he gibed, "with you in your pretty white dress."

"I cannot perform a ceremony against the young lady's will," the priest said valiantly.

"Oh, but she is very willing," Adam said softly. "She doesn't want the deaths of two soldiers and a number of Pawnee squaws on her already grubby little conscience. Do you, my love?"

She shook her head mutely, praying that Paul Sinclair would draw his pistol and shoot her, but he went on staring at her, not moving or speaking.

"Let us begin, then," Adam said softly. "I have no ring—"

"I have!" Deborah wrenched it from her finger and threw it down before him. It rolled a little on the stone and clinked into silence at his feet. He bent and picked it up, glancing at her from under his thick lashes as he said slowly, "So you found it. I forgot I put it in the pouch."

"You killed them." Eyes huge in her white face, she accused in a whisper.

"Because I loved you." He gave a short, bitter laugh and turned again to the priest, raising his voice harshly as he demanded, "The bride is willing! Come, begin the ceremony!"

CHAPTER
ELEVEN

SHE had stumbled out of one nightmare into another. In a daze she heard Father Purcell's voice, heavy with disapproval. "Dearly beloved, we are gathered here in the sight of God and this congregation to join together this man and this woman in holy matrimony—"

Paul Sinclair stood, the frozen look still on his face, as the service went on. Adam was making the responses and Deborah heard her own voice, dull and flat. The ring was thrust back on to her finger, and the watching Commanches made a mockery of the white bridal gown and the tranquil altar.

"I now pronounce you man and wife."

The words rang hollowly in the empty shell of her mind. Then Adam was signing the licence. Her own hand trembled violently as she scrawled her name, and she shrank back as two of the Commanches approached to make their mark as witnesses. Adam took the licence and seized her wrist, gripping it bruisingly.

"The rest of you wait here," he said curtly, and turned towards the side door, pulling her with him.

It was futile to resist. She went silently, biting her lip lest she cry out with the pain of the grip on her wrist. In the priest's bedroom he slammed the door, and pushed her away from him so violently that she stumbled to her knees.

"Get up! This is no time for praying!"

"Praying!" She pulled herself up and faced him. "I would like to kill you right this minute! I hope lightning strikes you stone dead! I hope—"

"Save your good wishes!" he broke in.

"I hate you! I never hated anyone so much in my whole life! You're a savage, a cruel murdering savage and they ought to lock you up on a reservation and throw away the key!" she blazed.

"One day they may do that, if they ever catch me," he said calmly. "But for the moment I intend to enjoy my – what do they call them? – marital rights."

"Don't come near me," she warned. "One step and I swear I'll kill you."

"By strangling me with your sash, I suppose? Don't act like a fool. At least let me explain—"

"You killed them! Murdered them! There's nothing you can say about that and nothing I want to hear."

"Is that dress yours?" he interrupted.

"What!" Checked in midstream, she glared at him. "It's one that belonged to the priest's mother, but why talk of dresses?"

"You had better take it off unless you want to get it torn."

"Take it—? I'll take nothing off!"

"Then I must do it for you. A pity to rip such a fine gown." He was smiling, his black eyes glinting in a way that terrified her more than any outburst of temper could have done.

With trembling fingers she began to unfasten the dress, stepping out of it and facing him with a nervous defiance, her arms crossed over her breasts, her hair falling over her shoulders in a riot of fiery curls.

"Take the rest off too," he said.

"I will *not*!" She backed away, her eyes closing with terror as he strode forward, his hands reaching to tear her undergarments.

"Don't faint," he said harshly. "You are not the swooning type."

"If you make love to me you'll get no joy of it." She was shaking so much that she could barely articulate the words, but as his mouth fastened upon hers she jerked away, hitting out with her fists, sinking her teeth into his wrist. He raised his hand and gave her a slap that brought tears to her eyes.

"Love! You need a good beating!" The pulse throbbing at his temple was more frightening than the paint on his face. She tried desperately to edge away, but he was upon her, lifting her, letting her dangle helplessly in his grasp for an instant, and then crashing her down upon the bed with such force that the breath was knocked out of her. Moaning, she tried to twist away but his body pinned her down, his teeth bit into her lips, his hands traced the curves of her writhing body.

"Goddamn you!" Deborah's scream was stilled in her throat as he wound his hands in her hair, shaking her to and fro. Long, slow quivers were creeping along her nerves, tingling her flesh, blurring the pain. Her small hands, beating against his back, were pulling him closer. Her whole body was turning traitor, and her mind raged helplessly against the sensual delight that drove all terror from her flesh.

"Adam! Adam!" Her voice soared up and then reality flooded her.

He had murdered the Laycocks in order to force her into marriage with him. An Indian marriage had no validity in law, and so he had forced her to go through the Christian ceremony before he raped her. Shuddering, she forced her body to match the revulsion in her mind, stiffening her muscles, clenching her fists against the almost overwhelming desire to hold him more tightly.

"You think the pretty Captain will pleasure you as I did?" he gibed.

"It was no pleasure," she whispered.

"You lie! I can see it in your eyes," he said.

"You can see nothing except hate." She closed her eyes, willing contempt into her voice, feeling his weight heavy on her. Little drops of sweat streaked the paint on his face and his voice was softly menacing.

"You think you can close me out of your heart so easily? I tell you that you cannot. I am locked into your soul, my woman, and without me you will be less than yourself."

"I never want to see you again," she said stonily. "I never want to see your face, or hear your voice, or endure your touch again."

"Because you fear your own instincts." He raised himself on his elbows, peering down into her face. Through her lashes she glimpsed his face, the eyes still mocking, the mouth curved into a smile that hesitated on the edge of tenderness.

She gritted her teeth against her own weakness and said, her tone coldly accusing, "You took me by force and now you expect me to thank you for it? You can go to hell!"

He moved away so swiftly that for a moment she feared he was rearing to strike her again, but he was merely adjusting his buckskins. His shadow fell across her as she lay spent on the rumpled covers, and she thought with a sudden and infinite sadness that his very existence had darkened all the years ahead.

"One day you will come seeking me," he said, not looking at her. "You will come, hungering for me, begging me to love you. When you have tired of soft beds and long gowns you will come seeking."

"Not in a million years!"

"I know you better than you know yourself." He turned and looked across at her and his voice started echoes in her mind. "You will come seeking, and I cannot promise what you will find."

If she spoke now he would come back and, taking her in his arms, be again the tender lover she had known. But if she spoke she would be giving tacit approval to the murder of the Laycocks.

He stood an instant longer, watching her with a peculiarly intense gaze, but she stared back in silence, her lips pressed tightly together, her heart hammering. Then he turned and walked out, closing the door softly behind him.

If she called him back now he would come. She ached with the wanting to call him back, even though she hated everything he had done. He was no better than a savage, less than any of the Indians she had met, for he had been educated and should have learned how to control his baser instincts. Unconsciously she strained her ears for the sound of hoof-beats, but if there were any the thick walls muffled them, and the silence around her was like a little death.

There was a tapping on the door and Father Purcell's voice sounded. "Child, are you all right? Are you hurt?"

"Give me a moment!" She raised her voice, keeping it steady with an effort.

"Are you hurt?" he repeated.

"No, no, I'm not hurt!" She scrambled from the bed and reached for her clothes, pulling them on over limbs grown chilly and stiff, putting on the grey gown in which she had arrived. Her wrist was throbbing and the mark of Adam's fingers showed up clearly on her white cheek.

When she opened the door, Father Purcell hurried to lead her to a chair, and to press a tin mug with whisky in it into her hands. From the other side of the room Paul Sinclair said, in a high, strained voice, "I ought to have killed him, you know! I shall always blame myself for that."

"We would all have paid with our lives," Deborah said wearily, and gulped the whisky shudderingly.

"My dear child, how did you come to be involved with such a man?" Father Purcell said. "He knew your name. He spoke as if he had been – on the most intimate terms with you!"

She was silent, her head drooping over the mug.

"Miss Debbie, I do feel that I have the right to know," Paul said gently.

"Yes, yes, of course." She raised her head and met his eyes shrinkingly. "I was married to him in a Navajo ceremony more than a year ago. I thought – I thought we might be happy, but then I found out his true nature. He has no heart, no conscience, no respect for human life. I left him, and I hoped never to see him again. I never will see him again."

"Child, he's your husband in law. I just married you both," Father Purcell said.

"A forced marriage! Surely—"

"Did he abuse you?" the priest interrupted. "Forgive me for my bluntness, but from the marks on your face, I take it that you were forced."

She nodded without speaking.

"And in the beginning, did he force you then?"

"I thought him different," she said, choking on a sob.

"Many brides are cruelly disillusioned after the wedding day. That does not invalidate the legality of the marriage."

"An Indian ceremony?" she queried desperately.

"Such a marriage is legal, provided both parties entered into it of their own free will," Father Purcell said.

"I'll not live with him," she flashed. "I never want to see him again!"

"The law doesn't force you to live with him," Father Purcell said. His tone was kindly, but there was reproach in his plump face.

"You ought to have been frank with me, Miss Debbie," Paul Sinclair said. "I offered you marriage in good faith."

"And I intended to be a good wife," she said miserably. "I never thought I would see Adam Leap-The-Mountain again."

"He is a handsome man," Father Purcell said thoughtfully. "There was good breeding in that face."

"He is a murdering Irish half-breed!" Deborah exclaimed.

"Irish, is he? Ah, that explains the breeding," the priest said solemnly.

"All this is quite pointless," Paul interrupted frostily. "Whatever the man's background, it seems clear that he is Miss Deborah's legal husband."

"I'll not go back to him!" Her voice splintered into panic.

"My dear child, nobody is going to force you to that," Father Purcell assured her, "but something has to be done with you. I can't possibly allow you to remain here. There's no other white woman for miles, and that man, having been here once, is quite likely to find his way here again."

"Couldn't your uncle—?" Paul began.

"I never had an uncle. That was just a story," Deborah said, defeated.

"Then forgive me, Miss Debbie, but perhaps it would be wiser if you did return to your – husband," Paul said.

There was deep offence in his expression, and she supposed that he was justified. He had been ready to marry her, and she had used him to further her own intentions. She had lied to him completely unscrupulously, and now she deserved his contempt. But to ride after Adam was something she would never do. She would die before she humbled herself before the man who had killed the Laycocks, and forced her to submit to him.

"I doubt if that would be possible now," Father Purcell said. "These Indians melt back into the landscape whenever they choose."

"I shall go on to Fort Laramie," Deborah said, breaking in. "There isn't anywhere else for me to go now."

"I cannot possibly be responsible for your safety during the remainder of the journey to Laramie," Paul said. "These natives can apparently descend upon us at any time, and on another occasion it's possible that some of my men will be hurt."

"He'll not come after me," she said.

"Can you be certain of that, child?" the priest asked.

"Absolutely. He won't come." There was the suspicion of tears in her voice. Hearing it, she drew a deep breath, raised her chin, and said, "So if you will be so kind, sir, as to allow me to ride with you to Laramie, I will seek employment there and not trouble you again."

"This is a most difficult situation," Paul said unhappily. "I offered you marriage in good faith, Miss Debbie. I admit it was not an affair of great passion, but my feelings for you were of genuine respect and affection."

"It might be possible to have the marriage set aside as null and void," Father Purcell said thoughtfully. "If he deceived you into the first ceremony—"

"What difference would it make?" She met Paul Sinclair's

gaze and asked, "You wouldn't want to have me as your wife now, would you?"

"It is not a matter of wanting." His fair skin reddened. "I have my career to consider – my promotion, Miss Debbie, and there is my family back in Boston. They are not narrow-minded people, but I must think of their feelings, of their standing in the community."

"You don't have to explain." She felt sorry for him as he sat there, twisting the tin mug he held round and round in his hands. "I am not the ideal bride for you to introduce to your family and friends."

"And an annulment would be difficult to obtain even under the present distressing circumstances," the priest agreed.

"But I'm not going back to *him*," she repeated stubbornly. "I would rather die than go back to him!"

"Now that's foolish talk!" Father Purcell said severely. "You must not make statements you don't mean. Death is a very serious matter, not to be desired before its due time!"

"I will go to Fort Laramie then," she said, "with or without the Captain's escort."

"Naturally I will escort you," Paul said. "The trouble is that I cannot hope to keep your story confidential. My men are aware that we came here with the intention of getting married, and the two who were overpowered by the Comanches cannot be expected to keep the story to themselves."

"I was forced against my will. There's nothing to be ashamed of in that," Deborah said.

"No, of course not. It is only that the other ladies—" Paul looked unhappy.

"Damn the other ladies! I care nothing for their opinion." Ignoring their shocked expressions, she rushed on, her voice growing shriller, "You look at me as if I were the one to blame. I was tricked into marriage the first time and forced into it the second time, by a man who has neither heart nor conscience. I have been assaulted and abused, and all you can think about is what the Laramie Sewing Circle will say if I arrive there under your escort. Well, they may say what they please and you may make what explanations you choose, but I am not going to crawl about apologising for the rest of my days! I am going to Fort Laramie, with or without your help, and I'm never going to see Adam Leap-The-Mountain again as long as I live!"

Abruptly she sat down again on the seat from which she had risen and burst into a storm of weeping. Over her head the two men regarded each other uneasily. Then Father Purcell, plump face creased in concern, said, "Nobody blames you, child. This is a most unfortunate affair, but you are young and time heals – yes, indeed, time heals most things."

"Naturally you may rely on my escort," Paul said uncomfortably. "I am sure you will find Colonel Maynadier to be most sympathetic when he hears your story."

"Then let us go back to the wagons." Deborah rubbed her eyelids with the corner of her shawl and sniffed.

"You are welcome to stay and rest," Father Purcell offered.

"I think it wiser if we leave the area as quickly as possible." Paul rose also. "I will have to make a full report to the Colonel."

"If you need my deposition it will be available." The two shook hands and then Father Purcell turned to Deborah. "This has been a terrible experience for you," he said. "It is a great pity that you did not confide fully in the Captain in the beginning, but one can understand your reluctance. I will pray for you, and for Adam Leap-The-Mountain."

"He needs no prayers," she said fiercely.

"We all need them," Father Purcell said, "and he must have desired you very greatly to take the risk of coming here."

"Desired to hurt and humiliate me," she flashed.

"Then he certainly needs prayer. Hate is an uncomfortable bedfellow." He shook hands with her, looking as if he would have liked to say more.

The troopers, one sporting a black eye, were already mounted. As Paul assisted Deborah to her horse she felt intense curiosity as well as sympathy directed at her by the two men, then one of them leaned to say, "Ma'am, we are surely sorry for what happened. Them Redskins jumped us afore we had a chance, and them Pawnee squaws just ran!"

"Thought my hair was gonna be lifted for certain," the other said. He had the air of a man who is still pinching himself to make sure he is alive.

"Thank you again, Father, and my apologies for this most unfortunate occurrence." Paul's face was scarlet.

He certainly had the gift of understatement, Deborah thought sourly as they rode away from the Mission. An embarrassed silence had fallen upon the little party, and from time to time she glanced around, half fearing, half hoping, to see the tip of a feather. There was nothing, however, but the broad track and the surrounding hills.

"It's asking a great deal of you, ma'am," Paul said awkwardly as they came within sight of the wagons, "but I'd like to move on immediately. We can make five or six miles before dark. I know they're gone, but I'll feel a lot happier when we're further from the Mission."

"I'm quite ready to travel." Deborah's voice was indifferent, her bruised wrist throbbing dully. Adam would be sorry if he knew he had hurt her, she thought, and then corrected the thought. Adam was a savage, a brute who had taken great delight in hurting her. Fortunately it was unlikely that she would ever see him again. More tears welled up in her eyes and coursed slowly down her cheeks, and she bent her head to hide them.

What Paul told the rest of his troop was something she never knew, for she went at once to the supply wagon that had been fitted up as a bed for her and burrowed under the covers, welcoming the cool dark. She could hear the murmur of his voice and a couple of shocked exclamations, and then the barking of commands as the horses were hitched up again. The rolling of the wagon wheels ground into her troubled mind, and she slept fitfully, and woke, one hand reaching for Adam even as she remembered that he was gone and that she hated him.

They pitched camp on the banks of a narrow river, and she gazed in longing at the water, wishing that she could strip off all her clothes and enjoy a good soak. Her dress felt too tight and her hair was in a confusion of tangles.

"Miss Debbie, the Captain sends his compliments and wonders if you'd prefer to eat supper in the wagon."

She blinked up at the thick-set trooper who had bent beneath the canvas hood.

"The Captain thought that you might feel – well, on account of what happened. You were – abused, and by a half-breed too!"

"You think it would have made a difference if I'd been attacked by someone else?" She sat up, pushing back her hair.

"White men don't abuse white women," he said, scowling.

"Indian squaws being another matter, I suppose?" She gave him a look of dislike. "You may inform Captain Sinclair that when I have tidied myself I will join him for supper. I certainly don't intend to spend the remainder of the journey hidden in the wagon."

"Yes, ma'am." The trooper gave her a look in which unwilling respect and salacious curiosity were mingled. "It was only that we figured you might not want to be seen in public just yet. Some of the others are talking."

"About what?"

"About this half-breed being your real husband from way back, and you not being too upset when he turned up. You see, ma'am, most young ladies in your position would have screamed or fainted. I knew of a girl who was taken by a Cree brave once, and abused. She killed herself so as not to bring shame on her family."

"Well, I'm sorry not to be able to oblige everybody,"

Deborah said crisply, "but I've no intention of killing myself to satisfy the conventions, and I'm way past the screaming and fainting stage. Perhaps you'd be good enough to send someone with a bucket of water? I am somewhat travel-stained."

"Yes, ma'am." The trooper still hesitated, eyeing her slyly, and said, "It's only that – some women are said to enjoy the embraces of these savages. We did wonder—" His voice trailed away.

"You are impertinent," she said coldly. "And I've no intention of gratifying your dirty-minded curiosity. Now get out, before I report you to Captain Sinclair, and send someone else back with the water!"

"Only wondered, ma'am. No need to get uppity about it!" He gave her another gown-stripping stare and ducked down into the gloom again.

Her tiredness had vanished and she was trembling with indignation. She had forgotten how people regarded white girls who had been taken by Indians and later returned. Many of them, she knew, were disowned by their families. Few of them could hope to make a respectable marriage. Yet a man could take an Indian mistress, discard her whenever he pleased, and be accounted something of a lad by all his friends.

And Adam must have known that when he left her behind and rode off with the Commanches. Perhaps he had hoped that the shame of her situation would drive her back to him. If so, then he was sadly mistaken, because she was ashamed of nothing.

Twenty minutes later, her face clean, her hair sleeked down, Deborah climbed down into the fresh air and marched resolutely to the small fire by which Paul Sinclair was sitting. He rose at once as she approached, bowing, and though the shifting firelight made it hard for her to distinguish his expression, his voice betrayed embarrassment. "I thought you might choose to remain under cover, Miss Debbie."

"Out of sight, out of mind?" She sat down on the proffered

stool, and accepted the tin plate with its inevitable mixture of jerky hash and beans.

"To spare your feelings, ma'am."

"The only feelings I have are gratitude for your kindness, and the determination to survive on my own terms without hiding away from the rest of the world," she put in.

"Then allow me to express my admiration, ma'am. You display great courage, and may count on my friendship," he said promptly.

"You are a nice person, Paul Sinclair," Deborah said softly. "I hope fortune sends you a rapid promotion and a pretty wife you can take home to Boston."

"And for myself," she added silently, "I can only wish for a speedy forgetting."

The soldier who could play the guitar had begun to strum softly again, the placid notes drowning the whispering voices of the men. They were probably discussing her, speculating as to whether her recent experience had made her easy game for any unscrupulous male. A few yards away the rising moon coaxed silver from the river and one of the ponies neighed restlessly. She raised her head, listening, her heart beating faster, but there was no other sound. Tonight no coyote called from the surrounding hills.

CHAPTER
TWELVE

"ONE hundred dollars and twenty-five cents!" Deborah made the final neat entry in the big accounts ledger and laid down the pen, stretching her arms over her head and yawning as she did so. She had been adding up figures for the last couple of hours, and her eyes ached.

"That's not a bad profit," Seth Ward said, rising from his chair in the corner and going to peer over her shoulder. "You sure you added up right?"

"Do I ever make a mistake?" she countered.

"No, ma'am. For a female you've a smart head," the trader admitted.

"And no heart at all," he added silently, frowning after her as she crossed to the window and looked out over the bleak landscape. She had been at Fort Laramie for almost a year now, and apart from the fact that she had a half-breed husband somewhere he knew no more about her than when she had ridden in with a detachment of troopers and asked him for a job. He still wasn't sure why he'd given her one, unless it had been a certain look in her big green eyes that reminded him of a little girl he'd been sweet on once back east. The girl had married somebody else, and he couldn't even recall her last name, but he'd found himself giving the newcomer a job, without even bothering to consult his partner, Butler, who was off on a hunting trip on Smoky Mountain. Two dollars a day and her keep, and she'd been worth every cent. The store was now making a handsome profit, the goods attractively arranged on the pine shelves, the stocks regularly checked and the books immaculately kept. She was a good-looking female, too, her red curls held at the back of her head with a black velvet bow, her green skirts held out over modest hoops, her green bodice filled in above high-pushed breasts with white net. Yet there was no yielding in her smile, no softness in her clear voice. During her months at the fort she had made no friends among the ladies, and the few men who had attempted to flirt had been repulsed with icy contempt.

Now, in a coaxing voice, moved by some obscure impulse of pity, he said, "Would you care to step over to my quarters, Miss Debbie, and take some supper?"

"Another time, Mr. Ward. I'm a mite weary this evening." She spoke politely, not turning from the window.

"At least the snow has stopped."

"It would be warmer if it did snow," she said, moving her slim shoulders restlessly. "The creek is iced over."

"It'll slow up the negotiations," he said gloomily.

"Do you think there is a chance of peace with the Sioux?" she asked.

"Possibly with the Brulé Sioux, but a treaty's not worth the paper it's written on unless Red Cloud of the Oglalas agrees, and he's not likely to take kindly to any agreement that allows whites unlimited access to the Black Hills."

"Whirlwind told me that some of the chiefs are on their way in to talk terms," Deborah said.

"If Whirlwind says so you can rely on it. That Indian is a walking news agency," Ward said. "Well, if you're tired I'll bid you goodnight. You'll remember to lock up?"

He said the same thing every night and she answered now, as usual, "I'll lock up."

"'Night then, Miss Debbie." Seth gave her a nod and went out.

Deborah had lit the lamp and a fire crackled in the hearth, but the pine-panelled room had a cheerless aspect. A worn rug took the chill from the floor and there were curtains at the window, a brightly patterned blanket over the narrow bed, but it was still just a room where she had not yet begun to sink her roots.

For a moment desolation swept over her. It was a loneliness that came when the sun had set and the bustle of the store had died down. At the other side of the compound lights blazed from the windows of the saloon bar, and further along she could see the raised planking outside the married quarters where a solitary guard patrolled.

Fort Laramie had no stockade to defend its rectangle of timber buildings, and the big wooden gates stood open. It was unlikely to be attacked, however, for too many friendly Indians lived in the surrounding meadows, their tepees pitched cheek by jowl with the wooden buildings of the military. There was a constant to-ing and fro-ing between the two communities and, watching the bright-faced young squaws jesting with the enlisted men, Deborah found it hard to realise that they lived in fact on a powder keg which might explode at any moment.

The little bell fixed over the main door jangled. Stifling a sigh, Deborah pushed open the inner door, calling, "I'm sorry, but we're just closing. I was lock—"

Adam-Leap-The-Mountain stood within the door, his hand still on the latch, his eyes fixed on her face with such astonishment that for an instant hysterical laughter bubbled up into her throat.

"You here!" His voice, harsh with shock, echoed around the store. The bell jangled again as he shut the door behind him and advanced towards her.

"Keep away from me!" Deborah backed away into the inner room, one hand in front of her to ward him away. "Don't come near me!"

"What are you doing in this place?" he demanded, ignoring her interruption. "I imagined you would have gone back east months ago."

"I was on my way to Laramie," she said on a high, breathless note. "I saw no reason to change my plans."

"Are you *working* here?"

"Yes, I am. Not that it's any of your business," she said childishly.

"You talk like a fool," he said calmly. "You're my wife and what you do is my business."

"*Wife!* You think I'm going to acknowledge that – farce you put me through?"

"It was a legal ceremony. I still have the licence," he mocked.

"Frame it and hang it on the walls of your adobe," she advised sweetly, "but lay one finger on me and I swear I'll scream the place down. They'll hang you."

"For assaulting my own wife?"

"Forced into marriage, tricked into marriage – don't touch me!"

"I wasn't going to touch you. I told you once that you would come to me one day. I'll not come to you."

"Yet you seem to be here." Now it was her turn to mock, and she ventured to do so though her voice still shivered on the edge of fear.

"By mistake. I rode in with Swift Bear and Standing Elk. We're camped further down the river."

"For the treaty talks?"

"I came to buy some tobacco," he said, his lip curling wryly.

"Have it as a gift!" She took a tin from one of the shelves and threw it at him. "And get out of here! Right this minute!"

"We have to talk." Adam picked up the tin and stood at a little distance, looking at her. In imagination she felt his hands gentling her into surrender and for a brief instant closed her eyes, fighting against the desire that surged through her loins; forcing into her mind the picture of the burning wagon and the faces of the Laycocks.

"I'll be over at the Sioux camp." His voice came to her from a long way away, and the bell jangled as he opened and closed the door again.

"Adam?" Deborah whispered his name, her hands reaching to grip the edge of the counter. She was shaking from head to foot. His sudden appearance, the well-remembered voice and lean face, had had upon her the effects of a crushing blow. After a long time she went over and locked the door, pulled the blinds down over the windows, and went back into the inner room. The fire was guttering low but she sat for a long time, staring into its embers, trying not to think of Adam.

"They're really beginning to crowd in," Seth Ward told her, strolling in the following morning.

"Who?" She glanced up from the pile of cotton reels she had already counted twice.

"The Indians, of course. Most of the peaceable chiefs are here already, and Spotted Tail is on his way in. He sent word that his daughter's not too well, so he's travelling slow."

"Fleet Foot is coming? Oh, I shall like to see her again!"

"You know the girl?" He looked at her in surprise.

"I met her once," she said briefly.

Seth Ward gave her another puzzled stare. Deborah Jones had never confided in him about her past life, but now there was a note in her voice he had never heard before.

"They do say she's a pretty girl," he said cautiously.

"Yes. Yes, she's very lovely," Deborah said. Her voice was cool again, her head bent over the cotton reels. Seth stared at her a moment longer and then went out again, whistling between his teeth, pushing his slouch hat to the back of his head.

The store was more crowded than ever that day. Many of the visiting Indians came in to buy tobacco or lengths of material for their wives, and stayed to gossip. Several of the officers' wives, eager to take a closer look at the newcomers, found that they had urgent purchases to make. Deborah was kept busy until midday, when she closed up for an hour and fixed herself a bite to eat.

Her feet ached from the long standing and her fingers quivered slightly as she poured out the coffee. Every time the bell had jangled she had jumped a little, her eyes flying to the door, but Adam hadn't come. Nobody had mentioned his name, and none of those who came into the store were known to her.

Drinking the coffee, she told herself firmly that she was delighted he had stayed away. With any luck he wouldn't come into the store at all. She clashed the cup back into the saucer, pushed away her untouched plate and rose, biting her lip, determined that she would concentrate on her work for the rest of the day and not allow one image of Adam-Leap-The-Mountain to intrude into her mind. Whatever had been between them was gone, destroyed by his own violence.

The day passed with intolerable slowness. She kept her mind on the purchases that were being made, noting them down, weighing flour and beans, giving change. At sunset the drumming began, a faint insistent pulsing below the clatter and bustle of the fort's activities. It grew nearer, ominous in its intensity. The flood of customers dwindled into a trickle and Deborah carried the overflowing cash-box into the inner room and began to pile up the coins, counting them aloud, her lips pressed tight with concentration.

It was no use. The compound was almost empty now save for a couple of pacing guards, and officers' wives, shawls flung hastily over their heads, were hurrying through the open gates towards the river crossing. Deborah went too, drawn by the urgent beating of the drums. The river-bank was crowded; braves, squaws and soldiers pressed closely together with no distinction of rank or person.

The Brulé Sioux rode and walked slowly towards the fort, the women with their braids unbound, the men with their faces painted black. In rank after rank they came, and in their midst, slung between two white ponies, a little, shrouded figure.

"Fleet Foot didn't survive the journey," Adam said. He had thrust a passage for himself through the crowd and stood near enough to embrace her, his face streaked with the black paint of mourning.

"Not now. Go away from me." Deborah muttered the words, her eyes on the swinging pall.

"Life is short, Laughing Flame," Adam said. "Come with me. There is still work to be done. Manuelito and Barboncito are holding out, and every month more of our people contrive to escape from the Bosque Redondo. Come with me."

He put his hand on her arm, his voice low against the beating of the drums. "I said that you would hunger for me, but I have starved for your company. Don't punish us both for a violence that is past. I'll wait two hours, no more. And if you don't come to me by then I'll not trouble you again."

She could not have spoken even if she had wished. A low wailing had broken out around her as the procession prepared to enter the compound, and the touch of his hand on her arm was lifted as he turned and went, cat-footed among the crowds.

"No." The one word was wrenched out of her and then she was running back towards the store, her skirts flying, her knuckles crammed between her teeth.

"Miss Debbie, whatever ails you?" Seth Ward had seized her by the shoulders and was shaking her.

"Fleet Foot is dead," she gasped, her eyes, wide and tearless, fixed on his own broad face without recognition. "Fleet Foot is dead."

"So they say." He looked down at her in frowning concern. "Is that what's upset you? Was she a particular friend of yours?"

"I met her once. She sang a song, of how the peace pipes came."

"They say she was regarded as a kind of princess among her own kind," Seth Ward said. "Colonel Maynadier has given leave for her burial platform to be erected in the military cemetery."

"She was a Christian," Deborah remembered.

"Are you all right now?" He released her from his grasp, still anxious, but the unseeing wildness had left her eyes.

"It was just the shock," she said vaguely. "I remembered her in a happier time, that's all."

When the young men had danced down the power of the

sun, and Magpie and I joined hands in the fertility ring. That was a wonderful day, before I found out that it was Adam who murdered the Laycocks.

"You sure you're all right?"

"Yes. Yes, I'm fine," she said remotely. "Excuse me while I go in and cash up. We made good profits today, and they'll increase the longer the treaty talks drag on."

"There'll be a bonus for you the end of the month," Seth promised.

"You're very kind." She gave him the same vague smile and hurried inside. The familiar store, its shelves depleted now, met her gaze.

"Miss Debbie, are you closed or can I buy some candy?"

One of the enlisted men had followed her in. He looked too young to be in the Army, his cheeks still round, his voice wavering uncertainly between alto and baritone.

"I've some candy left." She went behind the counter and rummaged in one of the boxes there.

"Everybody's going to the funeral," the boy said, handing over payment. "You going, Miss Debbie?"

"No. No, I don't think so."

"Colonel Maynadier's turned out the guard and lent his own chaplain. Seems she was an important sort of a squaw."

"Yes. Yes, she was."

"I saw her father ride in." The soldier clutched the candy. "Spotted Tail they call him. Big, fine-looking buck. You know what, Miss Debbie, he was crying just like he was a real person! You never saw anything to beat it. Crying, just like he was real sorry she'd died."

"She was his daughter."

"And he acted like he was – fond of her." The boy took a bite of the candy and said, cheek distended, "I think they've got feelings, you know. Like us."

"I think so too." She gave him an extra candy bar and smiled as he hurried out.

The accounts waited to be done. She tackled them with a kind of quiet ferocity, not thinking of anything but the coins before her, tensing her mind against unwanted emotion. The Laycocks had had feelings. They had been loving people, sharing a dream, and her months of fulfilment had arisen out of their brutal deaths. If she wavered in her resolution, if she went back to Adam now, she would be as guilty as he was.

The bell jangled again and she looked up through the open door as Spotted Tail came in, a blanket around his shoulders.

"Laughing Flame." He spoke her Indian name gravely and she answered him, "Spotted Tail."

"Star Chief Maynadier told me a Debbie Jones worked in the store. I hoped it was the same. Is Adam-Leap-The-Mountain with you?"

"No, he's not with me."

"I hoped for news of my Navajo friends. It is said they hold out still in the hills, but the pony soldiers hunt them down. We are here to make treaties, to put an end to the fighting. Many are making treaties with the whites. Black Kettle made one and the Star Chief gave him a big flag to put over his tepee."

"I'm sorry about Fleet Foot," she ventured.

"The river of my life is drained," he answered simply. "I have no heart left now for the fighting. She wanted me to make peace, you know. It was the last thing she asked."

"You'll have some coffee with me?"

"One cup and then I must return to the Star Chief," Spotted Tail said. "He's a good man. He speaks straight and his words make good sense. This is a fine store! You must be a very rich lady now."

"I work here, that's all."

"I still have much money," he told her. "I will give you some if you like."

"I have what I need."

"But you are not happy." He bent upon her a searching look. "You are not as I met you. I thought you would have a good life with Adam. He loved you as far as the stars, killed for you."

"I know."

"Not that anyone would weep for those Ute renegades. That was a wicked thing they did! A bad thing, to kill people who meant them no harm."

"Utes?" she said faintly. "*Utes?*"

"The ones who killed your people," Spotted Tail nodded. "Adam went hunting for them. They had some things they'd taken from the people they killed. A book with words on every page, and a ring—"

"A gold wedding ring." She stared at her hand.

"Adam got it back for you," Spotted Tail said, draining his coffee. "He told me about it. 'One day I will tell Laughing Flame,' he said. 'She hates killing, and she will be angry if I tell her too soon. But one day she will understand.' He told you, perhaps?"

"That he killed for love of me? Yes, he told me."

But she had assumed that Adam had murdered the Laycocks in order to trick her into marriage. It had never entered her head that it was the Utes who had suffered at his hands. Rough justice of which the Laycocks would have disapproved, but Adam had acted according to the customs of his father's nation. Punish your enemies and then forgive them! A harsh creed, but not a treacherous or disloyal one.

"If you marry a man you can hope to change him a little, but you must never expect to succeed," Mrs. Laycock had said to her once, and there had been a rueful smile on her lips. There must have been many times when she was weary of her husband's impractical schemes, of the constant travelling from place to place, the frequent dangers.

"Fleet Foot spoke of you," Spotted Tail said. "She made a little joke. She said, 'I have a red skin and a white heart, but Laughing Flame has a white skin and a red heart'."

"A Navajo heart," Deborah said slowly.

"I will make a big treaty and walk the white man's road," Spotted Tail told her.

"Will you excuse me? I – I have a treaty of my own to make," she asked abruptly.

"Later we will talk," he agreed.

"Later." She clasped hands with him briefly and ran out, the store door clanging behind her.

The compound was dim, but there were fires along the river bank and the scent of roasting meat wafted to her on the icy breeze. Small groups were huddled in their blankets around the flames and the drums still beat softly. The Sioux tepees were pitched near the river crossing. She ran towards them, her shoes slipping on the patches of ice, her breath white on the air.

"Adam! Adam!" Her voice was small on the rising wind and there was a stitch in her side. Startled faces, some streaked yet with black paint, looked up at her. She glimpsed Whirlwind and tugged his arm, her voice rising as her panic mounted. "Where is my man? Have you seen him?"

"Seth Ward's in the saloon bar, Miss Debbie."

"Not Seth, fool! Adam Leap-The-Mountain! The Navajo!"

"Tall, half-breed, buckskins?"

"Yes, that's Adam!"

"Rode in yesterday with Swift Bear?"

"Yes. Where is he camped? Which tepee?"

"He rode out an hour since," Whirlwind said, shaking his arm free.

"Rode out?" She stared at him blankly. "Rode where? Which way did he go?"

"Didn't say. Went south, I think – or west. I was rolling dice at the time."

"Did he – did he leave any message for me?"

"No, Missy. Just rode out."

"I see." She stood, arms leaden at her sides, the wind tousling her hair.

"You got any *minne wakan*, Missy?" a voice pleaded out of the darkness.

"No. No whisky. Store's closed," she said dully.

"You lose one man, take another," Whirlwind said, returning to his game.

"Will someone follow him, bring him back? I can pay – in

gold." Deborah gazed round desperately, but there were only a few uncomprehending shrugs in answer to her words.

"Maybe he come back pretty damn' soon," one of the squatting figures remarked.

"No. He won't come back. He won't ever come back again," she said, and the cold wind seared her to the bone.

Stumbling back, teeth clenched against a pain sharper than any stitch, she saw, high against the cloud patterned sky, the posts and platform of Fleet Foot's burial bed. The pall was roped to the platform and at each side of it, already covered by a thin layer of ice, were the two ponies, shot so that she could ride them in the Happy Hunting Grounds.

"Fleet Foot, tell me what to do!" She must have whispered the words aloud, but there was no reply. Only the wind moaned gently about the creaking platform and somewhere within the compound a lone bugler began to play.

CHAPTER
THIRTEEN

THE small office was stacked with documents and military manuals, leaving little space for a man to rest his elbows. Not that General Sherman was in the habit of resting any part of himself anywhere for very long. His Civil War had been an active one and, in the years since, he had travelled ceaselessly the length and breadth of the western states, alternately persuading and forcing various nations of the Indian peoples to relinquish their old hunting grounds. He was accustomed to harsh conditions, to long journeys in the rattling coaches of the expanding railroads, or in the high saddles of prairie-trained horses, but this place was as bleak as any he had ever seen. From the narrow windows he looked out over a sandy, treeless waste, its creek almost dried up, the fences patrolled by bored and irritable soldiers.

"Miss Deborah Jones to see you, sir." One of his orderlies had tapped at the door and now stood awaiting instructions.

"Who?"

"Miss Deborah Jones, sir. She has an appointment with you."

"To give evidence for the report of the Commission. I remember now. Tell her to come in." The General returned to his desk and sat down, his head bent over a sheaf of documents.

"Miss Deborah Jones, sir." The orderly stood aside as a small figure, her green skirts rustling around her, came in.

The General, glancing up indifferently, raised his eyebrows. The girl was young, her hair vividly red, her white skin unmarked by pox or sunburn. She was not pretty but her eyes were remarkable, their green flecked with gold, their lashes curling thickly above her cheekbones. It was a face of contradictions; the tip-tilted nose hinting at gaiety, the wide mouth set firmly above an obstinate chin.

"General Sherman?" She had planted herself in front of him, her head tilted back slightly, her clear voice challenging.

"Yes, madam." He looked up again, measuring her with his eyes.

"I do have an appointment. May I sit?"

Without waiting for an answer she lifted a pile of leaflets from a chair and sat down, her hands folded in her lap.

"So you are missionary at the Bosque Redondo? By whose authority did you come here?"

"By Colonel Maynadier's, sir."

"Henry Maynadier? You were at Fort Laramie, then?"

"Yes, General. I left the fort nearly a year ago and travelled south to the reservation with the new agent."

"Ah, yes. Norton." The General frowned slightly. "The man has done nothing but plague the Government with requests and complaints ever since he was appointed."

"And with good reason, sir," she interrupted. "Conditions at the Bosque Redondo are a disgrace to the conscience of the civilised world."

"Which is why I am here, to look into these conditions for myself."

"By staying within Fort Sumner and reading reports?" she enquired.

"Investigations must be carried out, madam," he said coldly. "Reports from various examining bodies have been compiled."

"I can see some of them." She flicked a pile with a small, contemptuous hand. "We've met these examiners too. Decent people, some of them. They click their tongues and tell us how sad it all is, and then they go away and write more reports. We are all suffocating under tons of papers, General. It's a pity you cannot change them into meat and give them to my people!"

"Your people?" He gave her an ironic stare that took in every detail of her appearance.

"In a manner of speaking, General."

"You are very young to be out here all by yourself," he said, tapping his teeth thoughtfully.

"I am twenty-two, sir."

"And you wear a wedding ring, though you call yourself Miss?"

"I was married once, sir."

"To a Navajo?" His look became even more puzzled, for she hadn't the appearance of a white squaw.

"He was half Irish, sir. Adam-Leap-The-Mountain. Perhaps you've heard of him?" Her voice was suddenly hopeful.

"Can't say I have. How did you come to be married to a Navajo half-breed?"

"It's a long story, General, and you are not here to enquire into my background," she said, her air of quiet dignity robbing her words of impertinence.

"As you say, Miss Jones." He nodded, not displeased at her frankness, and drew a sheet of paper towards him. "Now you have been here—"

"Eight months, sir. Before that I was at Fort Laramie, and prior to that I rode with Manuelito."

"Who finally surrendered last September," he said with satisfaction, "together with his remaining braves."

"Not all of them, sir." For a moment there was desolation in her voice, and then she became brisk again. "The fact is that I have lived with these people. They're a fine nation, with a heritage and culture of their own, settled on fertile land and cultivating it. The only reason for moving them was greed!"

"Western expansion must be encouraged," the General said stiffly. "The Indians are being granted new areas of land in compensation for the territory they have ceded."

"Such as the Bosque Redondo?" Angry colour rose in her face, and the words spilled out of her. "Nothing will grow here. Mr. Norton has tested the soil and it is alkali. Grain which is planted withers and dies in the earth. The water in the creek is brackish and there are very few trees. The people cannot build adobes fit to live in! They are not used to clay hogans, but to decent wooden houses. The Army sends us rations of bad flour and rancid bacon which their own soldiers refuse to eat! And we need medicines – quinine for the fever that sweeps through us like an evil wind when the warm days come."

"Supplies of whisky and tobacco—"

"Are no substitute for good food and sound buildings!" she interrupted fiercely. "The children need milk and fruit and fresh meat, and the women need spinning wheels and looms! Not whisky and tobacco!"

"I grant there have been blunders in administration."

"That is what you call them! I live out there, and I see each blunder as another death! The old and the very young die like flies from cholera and tuberculosis and the sweating sickness, and every month the Army commissioners come and count everybody and every month the numbers get fewer. One day there will be nobody left to be counted, and then you can recall the guards and tell the President there has been another blunder!"

She stopped, panting slightly, her eyes fixed stormily on the man who sat before her. His expression remained stern and brooding, and she wondered if anything she had said had moved him in any way at all.

"This husband you spoke about – is he dead?" he asked abruptly.

"I think he must be, sir. He was not with Manuelito when the warriors came in. I hoped he might be with the Sioux or the Chiricahua. George Bent was a friend of his."

"I know the Bents," he interrupted.

"George and Charlie? Is George married yet?"

"To Black Kettle's niece, Magpie. Nice little squaw."

"So they had a happy ending," she said softly. "We get so little news here, with the tribes split and scattered, and new treaties being made and broken all the time. When General Carleton was recalled to Washington we hoped we might be allowed to go back to our own land."

"I have no authority to grant such a move without the consent of the Senate."

"The Senate is granting millions of dollars for the resettlement of the Indians, isn't that so?"

"These people have to be fed."

"At the Government's expense. The land they were driven from is fertile. They could support themselves without any help if they were allowed to return there. The Canyon de Chelly hasn't been settled by white farmers, has it?"

"Not to my knowledge," he said reluctantly.

"Then let us return there. Close down the Bosque Redondo and save the Government a great deal of money."

"For a female you talk sense," he admitted. "It's something to consider when I make my annual report to Washington."

"And while you are considering," Deborah said hotly, "more and more will die! Consider for long enough and there won't be anybody left to return! Not that it will concern you! A General must grow indifferent to pain and suffering."

"Now you disappoint me by talking like a fool," he barked. "You fret over a few thousand natives. I have seen death in its bloodiest form, faced it, sent others to it. Indifference is the one emotion foreign to my nature."

"Then send the Navajos back to their own land. Prove your good faith!"

"Madam, I don't need to prove anything to you," the General said stonily. "I am not answerable to you."

"You are answerable to the future," Deborah said, rising with a swish of green skirts. "If a people die your name will be remembered as the man who did nothing to prevent it. There's a fine epitaph for a man who boasts a conscience!"

General Sherman opened his mouth to tell her that the interview was at an end, but she had already bobbed a curtsey and was on her way out, indignation in every line of her little figure.

"A Tartar, sir!" His orderly had come in again and was gazing after the departing figure with wry amusement. "I've been making enquiries about her, General, but there's not much to be gleaned. If the Navajos know her history they're keeping it to themselves. Seems she turned up here last year and considers herself to be one of them. Calls herself a missionary, but hasn't been heard preaching yet. She just nags, sir. On and on in the same groove."

"Let the Navajos go back to their own land," the General said.

"Exactly, sir. The guards say she's more trouble to them than all the chiefs put together. Nag, nag. If she ever did have a husband it's my belief he ran off to escape her tongue-lashings."

"A formidable young lady," the General said thoughtfully. His eyes were puzzled, and into his hard voice had crept an unwilling respect.

Deborah, having left the office, went with swift, angry strides across the compound. She had had hopes of this new general, but she feared they were doomed to disappointment. No doubt he would file away more reports, make more statements, and nothing would be done.

"Miss Debbie, can you spare a moment?" One of the troopers was beckoning her and she went across to him, her heels tapping the sun-baked earth.

"What is it, soldier?"

"There's an Indian on the post, asking for you," the man said.

"How astonishing! There must be at least four thousand of them around here," she said.

"Not a reservation Indian, Miss. A good-looking fellow in buckskins. Says he's an interpreter, and asked for you."

Her breath caught in her throat as she stared at him and a sudden wild hope rose up in her. "Where is he?" she whispered.

"Back in the guard room, ma'am. I wasn't certain—" He was talking to empty air, for she had veered away from him and was running towards the long timber building, her skirts flying out behind her.

The tall, black-haired figure stood with his back to her, staring through the window. On the threshold she paused, one hand at her throat, and then he turned and for an instant her disappointment was so acute that her cry was one of anguish.

"Nino! Nino?"

"Miss Debbie, I hoped very much you would be here." He spoke gravely, in English.

"I thought you were with Adam," she said in bewilderment.

"No, Miss Debbie. When you left the Bosque Redondo I told him about it and he rode north to find you again, but I stayed with the Chiricahua. I went down into Mexico with them."

"You went to find Yellow Bird?"

"No, not Yellow Bird. That is over between us. She is a rich lady, a married lady."

"You look prosperous yourself," she said lightly, noting his expensively fringed and studded buckskins, the pearl ring on his finger, the high-heeled boots.

"I met a lady," Nino said. "A very rich Spanish lady not young. She is past thirty. But very pretty, very charming. She makes of me a lover and then her family descend upon us. Oh, but they are very angry! Very angry indeed! Some of them think I ought to be hanged, but Maria is a very strong-minded woman. So we have a very grand wedding, and now we live on a fine ranch! But I wonder about you, if Adam ever finds you."

"He found me," she said, her disappointment souring into a resigned bitterness. "He found me and then we parted. I saw him briefly about a year ago when the Brulé Sioux went to talk peace at Fort Laramie. Since then I've heard nothing."

"He didn't come in with Manuelito?"

"No. They were starved out in the end, no weapons, no hope. But Adam wasn't with them. Have you seen Manuelito and the others yet?"

"Better I don't," Nino said. His voice was sombre. "I have a Mexican home now, a Spanish wife. I have brought gold. Will it buy more food, more clothes?"

"Yes, it will." She took the heavy leather bag from him, her gratitude tinged with sadness. She was pleased that Nino had carved out a new and prosperous life for himself, but the eager boy who had pledged himself to Charity would never come again.

"You and Adam quarrelled?" he asked.

"I thought he had killed the Laycocks, the people with whom I was travelling," she said.

"Oh, no, Miss Debbie! He went out and found the Utes who had murdered them, and killed them for it. Only a few of us knew about it and we promised not to tell you. I have worried about that ever since you found the ring, but you did make me tell you, Miss."

"Yes. Yes, I did make you."

"Did it cause trouble between you and Adam-Leap-The-Mountain?" he asked.

"It wasn't your fault," she said. "This gold will be very useful, Nino. I'll see it's spent wisely. But don't you want to see your relatives? Little Coyote is a big boy now. I'm teaching him to read."

"No, I came simply to find out if you and Adam were here. I am going back to Mexico very soon."

"Your road took a strange turning. Are you happy, Nino?"

"Maria is a good wife," he said. "She is going to have a child soon. A fine son, or a daughter, eh? But you are not happy, Miss Debbie. There is no sunlight in your eyes."

"I am too busy to be happy," she said coldly.

"Did you wish me to seek Adam for you?" he asked.

"No." She shook her head, forcing a smile. "It is your

duty to look after your wife now, and to manage your ranch. We walk different roads, my friend."

"Then I wish you good fortune," Nino said, shaking his head as if he doubted whether it would come to her. "Are you living here now, Miss Debbie, on this reservation for the rest of your life?"

"No, of course not!" she said briskly. "General Sherman is here now, investigating conditions. I have every hope we will all be allowed to return to our own land. Every hope!"

"Yes, Miss Debbie." For a moment he was the lad who had followed her, his gaze trusting. Then he began to talk about his pretty Spanish wife again and the moment was past.

She watched him leave without regret, sending her good wishes after him. In a way, seeing him go was like closing a chapter.

The unfinished pages of her own life fluttered in her thoughts as she walked back down the stony track that led to the reservation proper. The somnolence of a hot afternoon lay over the barren earth. A few children counted coup in and out of the hogans of mud and straw. In one corner, shaded by a canopy of mesquite fronds, the chiefs sat in a circle, smoking and discussing old campaigns. A soldier, cap at an impudent angle, went past, whistling at two giggling girls.

"You spoke to General Sherman?" Juanita, patching a pair of trousers for Manuelito, called to her as she approached.

"I spoke to him." Deborah went over and squatted beside her. "He said nothing, and I said too much. I lost my temper, and told him just what I thought of these everlasting enquiries and commissions."

"They mean well," Juanita said tolerantly. "You must learn patience, child."

"Patience never got a Navajo off the reservation yet!" Deborah scolded.

"Many are contriving to slip away," the older woman said.

"And more remain here to die, or sink into apathy," Deborah countered. "I get so *angry* when I think of it."

"You are angry with yourself too," Juanita said, glancing shrewdly at her companion. "You punish yourself because you didn't go with Adam."

"Adam is probably dead by now. There's been no word of him."

"So, you shout at Generals and work until you drop, so that you will be too tired to weep for your man."

"I don't want to talk about it," Deborah said stubbornly.

"Pride is a bad bedfellow." Juanita snapped off a thread and held up the frayed garment, squinting at it critically.

"Let Adam come to me. I left word at Fort Laramie."

"Adam will not come. If you do not know that then you know nothing," Juanita said. "Will you stay here, growing old in this wilderness?"

"None of us is going to stay here," Deborah said, her green eyes sparkling with sudden determination. "I tell you, Juanita, we are all going home. All of us! I'll not rest until we get back to the Canyon de Chelly."

"And after that, if it ever happens?"

"It will happen. We'll make it happen!" she interrupted.

"And then what will you do?" Juanita asked.

"Then I'll seek for Adam," Deborah said slowly. "If he's alive I'll find him, even if I have to walk from one end of the land to the other. I'll not rest until the journey's done."

"You're a good squaw," Juanita said affectionately.

"And I'm going back to see the General right now," Deborah declared, jumping up and brushing the dust from her skirts. The dust was everywhere in this place, rising in clouds from the scorched earth, clogging the nostrils, powdering the skin. "I'm going back right this minute and this time I'll make him take notice of me! And you must get the women together. They sit about, feeling sorry for themselves, lacking even the energy to swat the flies! We'll have protest meetings, delegations! And the chiefs should draw up conditions on which they would be willing to sign a treaty!"

Her longing for Adam was so acute that it was hard to draw

breath comfortably, but she raised her chin and said fiercely, as if she were challenging the whole world, "We're going home again, Juanita. We're going home, no matter how long it takes!"

EPILOGUE

It had taken a further year, twelve months of argument and pleading, of interviews, and statements taken down by solemn-faced officials, and long hours of waiting to see various gentlemen who had travelled from Washington to see for themselves how conditions were at the Bosque Redondo. There were nights when Deborah was too weary to sleep and lay, tense and wakeful, staring up at the thatched ceiling of her hut, and mornings when she felt almost too dispirited to drag herself out of bed to begin yet another day's struggle against the stupidity of bureaucrats, the constant hunger and sickness and lack of fresh water and medicines. When she thought of Adam it was with a frustrated longing for everything they had once shared, and a determined hope that one day they would share those things again.

"Well, Miss Jones, you have had your way," the General said brusquely when she went to say goodbye to him. "The chiefs have signed a perpetual treaty and in return your people are allowed to return to their own land."

"An honourable decision, sir, which reflects great credit on you," she said, "though it comes very late. The Navajos should never have been sent to the reservation at all."

"The original decision was not mine," he reminded her, "and you have been free to leave at any time."

"Only in law," she said, smiling faintly.

"Will you travel back with them?" he asked curiously.

"Yes." She hesitated, then said, flushing slightly, "I have another matter to attend and I have promised myself that I will begin it soon."

"Oh?"

"I have – someone to find," she said, and rose, shaking hands briskly, with a look on her face that precluded further questioning.

After all their struggles the journey back was a simple, quiet affair, with no wild celebrations to mar its dignity. They rode and walked in long columns, the children strapped to their mothers' backs, the old people crammed into the few carts and wagons the Army had spared, the chiefs on horseback, their faces smeared with the yellow and white of hope, their tails of hair bound with red, gold rings glinting in their ears. Five thousand people, and not one of them turned to look back.

"Four years since we were attacked at the Canyon de Chelly," Juanita said. "Does it seem longer than that to you?"

"It seems like a lifetime," Deborah said wearily. "I feel about a hundred years old!"

"It will be good to be back." The chief's wife slanted a questioning look at her and said, "You will not stay with us though?"

"For a few days only. Then I will ride out again."

"To seek Adam-Leap-The-Mountain?"

"If he still lives. I cannot tell."

"Where will you seek?"

"Among the Chiricahua. It's likely they will know."

"They may not tell you," Juanita warned. "Cochise has little reason to help the white man now, and your fire hair could prove tempting to his warriors."

"I still have to go," Deborah replied. "I have to be sure, Juanita."

"Yes." Juanita nodded, her dark eyes understanding and said again, "Yes."

They were making good time despite the scarcity of horses and the steadily increasing summer heat which shimmered up from the reddish rocks, creating mirages of fair palaces and rainbow towers out of the windswept mesas. To be going home again was an unspoken song in every heart, and each sunset was a further stage upon the journey.

"Tomorrow we will reach the canyon," Manuelito told them as they pitched camp for the twentieth time. "We start at dawn and we ride singing. There will be a hunt and a feast. A big feast, with dancing and the children playing jokes and the old ones telling tales of their youth."

"And the braves getting drunk on the whisky the soldiers gave you, and everybody having bad headaches in the morning," Juanita said.

"You see how she treats me?" The chief pulled at his drooping moustache and winked over his wife's head. "She is worse than the guards at the Bosque Redondo."

"And they couldn't keep you in order either," Juanita said teasingly.

Abruptly Deborah rose and wandered away from them towards the creek near where they had halted for the night. It was not yet dark, and groups of people were settling down to eat their meagre rations and soothe the children fretful after the long day's march. Any of them would have greeted her and made room in their circle, but an unaccountable depression had fallen upon her. Their journey would soon be over. Hers would soon be starting again, and she shivered, picturing the long and perhaps fruitless quest. Kneeling at the water's edge she cupped her hands to drink, blinking as the last rays of sunlight splintered the surface of the creek into a thousand stars of dancing colour.

"We always meet where the waters run swift."

It was Adam's voice and, as she spun about, Adam's hand that pulled her from the brink, drawing her into the shadow of the rock.

"You are not dead," Deborah said foolishly, and stared at him as if she had just uttered a lie and he was some mirage come to haunt her.

"I rode with the Chiricahua. Then, six months ago, I met Nino again. He told me of your foolish mistake."

"Foolish! It was a natural misunderstanding!"

"A few questions would have saved us both much heart-ache," he said.

"Six months ago! Then you knew I was at the reservation! Why didn't you come for me?"

"Because I said that I would not."

Baffled, she gazed up at him, knowing in that moment that she would never fully understand this man in whom two races met and mingled.

"You are here now," she said at last, her voice small and uncertain.

"Because my father's people are going home again. Will you follow me?"

"I was going to come in search of you," she whispered. "I meant to seek you in every part of the land."

"And that too was foolish," he said gravely, "for you held me between your hands all the time. Will you let it drain away like moisture on the cactus flower when the sun rises, or will you drink down my life and so renew us both?"

There was no need for answer. His mouth was upon her mouth, his hands pulling loose her fiery mane of hair, his voice murmuring in sounds that were ancient before nations were divided. He lifted her and carried her along the river bank to where the sagebrush grew a tall screen to shield them from all eyes. Her green dress peeled from her like the stalk of some pale water flower and his warmth enfolded her, rousing a primitive answering fire that scorched to the depths of her being.

"I have seen the canyon," he said, voice harsh in the gathering shadows. "The adobes are ruined, and weeds grow tall where once there were peach trees. It will take many months, many years, to set right, and the winters will be harsh ones. Will you choose to share that with me? Will you make each moon of my life a moon of Laughing Flame? I can offer you nothing but the hope of a future, but you must choose now for us both."

"Listen!" She put her finger to his lips, raising herself slightly.

On the river bank a girl had begun to sing; probably in lullaby to a whimpering baby, but her voice was joined by others, humming at first then swelling from group to group.

"With visible breath I am walking,
A voice I send as I'm walking,
In a sacred way I am walking,
With visible tracks I am walking,
In a sacred manner I walk."

The Peace Pipe song, chanted at that far-off Sun Dance by the gentle Fleet Foot, rose into the evening air. The voices of a people that would not admit the possibility of defeat.

"Listen!" Deborah put her arms about him, drawing him down into her waiting sweetness. "Listen, my husband! Our people are singing!"

And the moon, rising higher into the sky, was girdled with the last brilliance of the sun, promising a bright dawn on the morrow.

Masquerade
Historical Romances

Intrigue excitement romance

Don't miss
January's
other enthralling Historical Romance title

THE ICE KING
by Dinah Dean

Prince Nikolai Volkhov is known at the Czar Alexander's court as 'the Ice King' — as famous for his cold reserve as for his lack of interest in feminine wiles. Why, then, should he seem to take such an interest in Tanya, a penniless orphan, almost on the shelf?

Snatching at her last chance of a little gaiety in St. Petersburg before she resigns herself to a bleak, hopeless future, Tanya no longer trusts in good luck. She knows that Prince Nikolai's attentions can mean nothing but heartbreak — because, like a fool, she has fallen in love with a man of whom she knows nothing . . .

Doctor Nurse Romances

and January's
stories of romantic relationships behind the scenes
of modern medical life are:

TENDER LOVING CARE
by Kerry Mitchell

Stephanie loved nursing at the little Australian country hospital, but why had Doctor Blair Tremayne suddenly turned against her?

LAKELAND DOCTOR
by Jean Curtis

It was only when the beautiful Lena came to the Lakeland village that Hilary understood why she had stuck for so long to her job as Doctor Blake Kinross's secretary!

Order your copies today from your local paperback retailer.

MARIETTA
by Gina Veronese

Marietta was the richest woman in Florence — but when she fell in love with Filippo, poor but proud, she discovered that her wealth counted for nothing ... It could not recover his lost inheritance, or save them both from danger.

THE REBEL AND THE REDCOAT
by Jan Constant

Events of the Scottish uprising in 1745 apparently proved Anstey Frazer a murderess. Yet, on the long and gruelling journey south to her awesome trial, she found herself increasingly attracted to the Redcoat captain who was her captor ...

Look out for these titles in your local paperback shop from 8th February 1980

Masquer
Historical Roma

Intrigu
exciteme
romanc

THE SHADOW QUEEN
by Margaret Hope

It was Kirsty's uncanny — and potentially danger
— resemblance to Mary, Queen of Scots, that save
her from an arranged marriage with Dirk Farr, the
gipsy laird. But had she only exchanged one peril fo
another?

ROSAMUND
by Julia Murray

Sir Hugh Eavleigh could not forget Rose, the enchant-
ing waif who had tried to rob him on the King's
Highway. Then he learned that she was really Lady
Rosamund Daviot — his prospective bride!

THE ABDUCTED HEIRESS
by Jasmine Cresswell

Georgiana Thayne was so determined not to be
married for her money that she pretended to be
plain and childishly stupid. It took an abduction by
the wicked Marquis of Graydon to make her show
her true colours . . .

These titles are still available through your local
paperback retailer.